The look in her eyes undid him.

Without giving her time to protest, Michael leaned forward and kissed her. The kiss was a celebration. A celebration that they were alive…and she was in his arms.

He devoured her with an urgency that no longer surprised him. No matter why he'd come to Jenkins Cove, everything had changed the moment he held Chelsea.

Strange things had been happening to him since he'd arrived. Things he couldn't explain in any of the rational terms he'd used all his life. Falling for Chelsea was no exception.

When he felt her body move against his, he forced himself to stop. They'd only known each other a few days, but he wanted her. More than he'd wanted any other woman. But he wasn't going to make love to her in the woods. And certainly not when the gunman they'd narrowly escaped was still out there… watching…waiting.…

REBECCA YORK

RUTH GLICK WRITING AS REBECCA YORK

CHRISTMAS SPIRIT

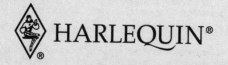

HARLEQUIN®

TORONTO • NEW YORK • LONDON
AMSTERDAM • PARIS • SYDNEY • HAMBURG
STOCKHOLM • ATHENS • TOKYO • MILAN • MADRID
PRAGUE • WARSAW • BUDAPEST • AUCKLAND

ISBN-13: 978-0-373-88863-4
ISBN-10:   0-373-88863-5

CHRISTMAS SPIRIT

ABOUT THE AUTHOR

Award-winning, bestselling novelist Ruth Glick, who writes as Rebecca York, is the author of more than one hundred books, including her popular 43 Light Street series for Harlequin Intrigue. Ruth says she has the best job in the world. Not only does she get paid for telling stories; she's also an author of twelve cookbooks. Ruth and her husband, Norman, travel frequently, researching locales for her novels and searching out new dishes for her cookbooks.

Books by Rebecca York

CAST OF CHARACTERS

Chelsea Caldwell—She'd tried to escape her past. But it came rushing back to her when she returned to Jenkins Cove.

Michael Bryant—He thought Chelsea was lying—or worse—and he meant to expose her.

Aunt Sophie Caldwell—Was she just a batty old woman who believed in psychic phenomena?

Chief of Police Charles Hammer—Was he lazy…or hiding something?

Ned Perry—Would the land developer kill to get his hands on prime real estate?

Dr. James Janecek—How did he fit into the Jenkins Cove puzzle?

Edwin Leonard—What was the butler so worried about?

Phil Cardon—Was he just a handyman? Or did he have sinister motives?

Rufus Shea—Could the tavern owner turn his sorry life around?

Franz Kreeger—Who was he working for?

Chapter One

Chelsea Caldwell drove through the fog-shrouded darkness, her hands gripping the steering wheel of her Honda as she leaned forward and struggled to focus on the road.

"Relax," she whispered to herself. "Tensing up isn't going to help."

She should have put her foot down. This wasn't an emergency trip. Aunt Sophie didn't need Christmas decorations tonight. Tomorrow morning would have been a better time to drive over to the craft shop on Tilghman Island.

But her aunt had been anxious to get a head start on the season. And Chelsea had forgotten how fogs could roll in from the Chesapeake Bay—or from the creeks and rivers that crisscrossed this part of Maryland's Eastern Shore.

That was proof of how much her life had changed in the past few months. She'd been living in Baltimore, well on her way to establishing herself as a sought-after local artist whose paintings were described as "haunting."

Now she was back in Jenkins Cove, the town where she'd spent her summers at the House of the Seven Gables, Aunt Sophie's sprawling Victorian bed-and-breakfast right on the town harbor.

Her aunt was getting on in years and could no longer run the B & B by herself. Chelsea knew that if her aunt was forced to sell the business she'd run for the past forty years, her reason for living would be gone.

Chelsea simply couldn't let that happen to her only living relative. So she'd done what she'd sworn she'd never do. She'd moved to Jenkins Cove.

Once, she'd loved the town and the House of the Seven Gables. Now it felt like foreign territory. She was struggling to settle into the rhythm of life in the quaint little community whose main business was tourism.

Every year the merchants sponsored a contest for the best and most tasteful holiday display. Aunt Sophie wanted to win—which was why she'd sought out a woman known for the specialty garlands she created and why the trunk of the car was full of holiday greenery.

Chelsea felt her shoulders begin to tense again. It was spooky along this stretch of four-lane highway. She could imagine ghosts weaving their way through the trees.

"Stop it!" she ordered herself, firming her lips as

she kept driving. "Don't think about that now. Just get home, and you can have a cup of hot chocolate in the parlor."

A car honked and passed. A fool going too fast for the foggy conditions.

When a noise in the trees to her left made her jump, she took her eyes from the road for a moment.

"It's only an owl," she muttered, then flicked her gaze to the blacktop again—just as her headlights illuminated a shape on the pavement. Gasping, she slammed on the brakes.

In the swirling mist, she saw what looked like a person huddled on her side, lying on the pavement. A woman with long dark hair fanned out behind her head.

Easing the car to the gravel shoulder, Chelsea sat with her heart pounding for several seconds.

Though she wanted to stay in the car where it was safe, she knew she had to get out and help the woman. With an unsteady hand she cut the engine, then reached toward the glove compartment and got out a flashlight.

Gripping the barrel like a club, she stepped out, shivering in a sudden gust of wind that rattled the bare branches of the trees. During the day, the weather had been warm for the last days of November, but after dark the temperature had sharply dropped.

After glancing up and down the highway, she

walked back toward the place where she'd seen the woman. But when she shone the light on the ribbon of macadam, she saw nothing.

"Hello? Where are you? Are you okay? Can I help you?" she called out.

When no one answered, her fingers tightened on the flashlight and her throat clogged. Maybe she'd been mistaken, she thought as she swung the beam along the road, then onto the far shoulder, the mist distorting the light.

As luck would have it, no other cars passed. With a quick glance back at her car, she walked along the shoulder, shining the light into the underbrush.

Again, nothing.

Finally, she returned to the vehicle and fumbled in her purse for her cell phone. But when she opened the cover, it made a beeping sound and went black.

She muttered something very un-Christmas-like under her breath and put the phone back. Who was she going to call, anyway? Police Chief Hammer? And tell him what? That she thought she'd seen a body on the road to Tilghman Island and now it was gone—vanished like a ghost?

The lazy old bulldog would really thank her for that.

Charles Hammer must have had some kind of pull to get voted into office. Too bad the town couldn't get rid of him for another couple of years.

Or maybe most of the people in Jenkins Cove thought he was doing a fine job.

After casting one last anxious glance at the spot where she thought she'd seen the woman, Chelsea started the engine again. The mist was thicker now, and she drove more slowly, afraid to hit a deer leaping across the highway.

Maybe that's what she'd seen earlier. A deer, hit and momentarily stunned. There hadn't been anybody lying on the blacktop, after all. It was just her imagination working overtime.

She'd started to relax a little when a flash of movement made her brake again.

This time she didn't see a body lying across the blacktop. This time, in the moonlight, she saw a woman running through the woods at the side of the road. And a man chasing her.

Her long black hair was streaming out behind her, and she looked as though she was wearing a dark coat that hung loosely on her body.

The woman screamed, then screamed again as the man caught up with her, catching her by the hair.

Chelsea pulled to the shoulder once more. Grabbing the flashlight again, she leaped from the car.

"Get away from her," she shouted as she charged into the underbrush.

She heard the woman whimper and thought she saw the man raise a knife. Then they both disappeared into a thicker patch of woods. When Chelsea tried to follow, she splashed into cold water that slopped over the tops of her shoes. As she pressed onward into sucking mud, she floundered into a water-filled hole and almost fell on her face. She was in one of the swampy areas so common around Jenkins Cove, and if she kept going, she was liable to end up waist-deep in freezing water.

Heart pounding, she stared into the bog. The woman and the man had vanished into the darkness as though they had never been there.

As Chelsea replayed the scene in her mind, she realized she'd never heard anything besides the woman's scream. Shouldn't they have been splashing through the water? And how had they gotten through the swamp, anyway, when she had ended up knee-deep in frigid water almost immediately?

She backed up, feeling her way carefully, trying not to step into another hole. She'd only been out of the car for a few minutes, but her pant legs were soaked, and her legs and feet already felt like blocks of ice.

As she retraced her steps, she wondered what she had seen. Had her overactive imagination combined with some trick of the moonlight to make her think that a woman was running for her life?

Chelsea made it back to her car and stamped her feet to shake off some of the mud. Climbing inside, she closed the door and sat behind the wheel, shivering.

She started the car and turned up the heater, thinking that she had to report this to the police.

Even if it turned out to be nothing. Even if the last thing she wanted to do was tell her tale to the cops.

She raised her head, looking around for a landmark. A few yards away was a sign advertising a restaurant in Jenkins Cove. Now she knew how to find this spot again.

While she stared at the sign and the blackness beyond, she thought about something that had happened when she was ten. Something she could block out of her mind most of the time. But not now.

She'd been at a friend's house out at Mead's Point, on a farm that bordered the bay. She and Amanda had been playing outside down near the water. When it got dark, neither one of them wanted to come in, so they went over to the old icehouse to look for fireflies.

That was where it had happened. Amanda was looking out toward the bay, while Chelsea was staring at the icehouse, trying to figure out why the shadows seemed so strange around the little building and why the air felt so cold.

Then a young woman stepped out of the doorway and stood facing Chelsea. She held out her hand, her face pleading as though she wanted something urgent.

Her lips moved, but Chelsea couldn't hear what she was saying. She only felt a terrible pressure inside her own chest and horrible waves of anguish coming off the woman.

She moaned or screamed something, because Amanda came running. But her friend didn't see anything.

When Chelsea looked up, the woman had vanished.

"She was here. I saw her," Chelsea insisted.

"You're making it up."

"No, I'm not. I saw her."

Maybe it was fear that made Amanda start teasing her.

"Liar, liar. Pants on fire."

The next thing Chelsea knew, she was in tears. She'd been looking forward to spending the night at Amanda's, but she was too upset for that. She ended up going back to the House of the Seven Gables, where Aunt Sophie did her best to find out what had happened and then to comfort her.

But Chelsea was beyond comfort. She knew with a strange certainty that the woman she'd seen was a ghost. A ghost who was depending on her to set things right—whatever that meant. But Chelsea simply hadn't been able to understand her. And she felt like a failure.

It was a lot to put on a ten-year-old girl. So much that the experience changed her whole feeling about Jenkins Cove. Until then, she'd loved spending the summer down on the Eastern Shore. It had been a child's dream vacation.

After that incident, though, she'd only come back for short visits with her parents—until they'd been killed in a car accident right after her senior year of college. Then she'd come back from time to time to visit Aunt Sophie, her father's older sister.

Now she was back in town again—for the time being.

At first she'd felt a vague sense of foreboding. When nothing upsetting had happened, she'd started hoping that living with Aunt Sophie would work out for her. She'd taken over a third-floor room in the House of the Seven Gables for her art studio, where she worked most days. She was still sending some paintings to galleries in Baltimore. She was also selling at some of the galleries on Main Street right here in town.

And now this.

But what was *this,* exactly?

She took her bottom lip between her teeth. Had she seen another ghost?

She didn't want to talk to anyone about it, least of all Chief Hammer. But she knew she had to—in case this was something real, and she could save the woman's life. Or help the police find her body. That last thought made her shudder.

With shoulders hunched, she drove into Jenkins Cove, past the town square and all the shops and restaurants to the side street where the police station was located. Once it had been housed in an ugly redbrick building on Main Street. Now it was on a parallel street and it looked like a two-story beige clapboard house with a gable in the center of the front, a wide front porch and a red front door.

Pulling up in the parking area beside the building, she sat for a moment, steeling herself, picturing the chief in his rumpled navy-blue uniform.

He'd been here fifteen years ago when she'd seen the ghost out at Mead's Point. He hadn't been in charge then, just one of the deputies. But, like everyone else in town, he heard about her ghost sighting. Back then, everyone was talking about her. Which was one of the reasons she'd wanted to get away from Jenkins Cove.

She tried to shove all that out of her mind as she climbed the three steps to the porch and pushed open the door.

Since it was after hours, the receptionist's desk was empty, but a light was on in the back, and Chief Hammer called out, "Who's there?"

"Chelsea Caldwell."

She must have sounded pretty shaky, because he came barreling out of his office, faster than she'd thought the squat bulldog of a man could run.

He took one look at her and helped her into one of the wooden chairs against the wall, his gaze taking in the water that sopped her shoes and slacks.

"What happened? Did you drive into a ditch?" he asked.

She shook her head. "No. It wasn't that. I...saw something when I was driving back from Tilghman

Island. I got out, but…then I stepped into a hole full of freezing water."

He looked at her through small blue eyes. "Take your time, and tell me what happened."

She gulped in air, then blurted, "First I thought I saw a body in the middle of the road."

The sharp look on the chief's face made her cringe.

"Thought you saw?" he asked.

"Well, I stopped, but there was nothing there. It was foggy, so I guess it was just a trick of the light. But then a little ways up the road, I saw a man chasing a woman through the bog."

"Where was this, exactly?"

"Near the sign advertising the Crab Pot. Do you know where I mean?"

"Yeah."

"I got out and chased them."

"Bad idea," he muttered.

"But I…" She stopped and pointed down toward her wet feet. "But I stumbled into a hole full of water. Sorry. I tracked mud all over your floor."

"Don't worry about that." He stood there staring at her and tapping his finger against his lips.

Holding herself very still, she waited for him to make a smart remark about the ghost she'd seen all those years ago.

When he finally spoke, he said, "It would help if you could come out there and show us the exact place where you saw the woman and the man."

She nodded. She'd hoped she could go home, now that she'd done her duty. But she knew he was right. "Okay."

He looked down at her wet shoes and pants. "We keep clothing at the station in case an officer needs to change. I hope you don't mind wearing uniform pants and rubber boots."

"Thanks. I'd appreciate it."

"While you change, I'll contact a couple of my deputies."

She waited while he produced a pair of navy-blue uniform pants and a pair of rubber boots. The boots were much too big, but three pairs of heavy wool socks helped hold them on her feet.

When she came out of the ladies' room where she'd changed, two uniformed officers were conferring with the chief. Hammer made the introductions but the deputies—Sam Draper and Tommy Benson—had little to say to her. She wondered what the chief had told them while she was changing her clothes. Had he confined himself to tonight's incident, or had he told them about her misadventure fifteen years ago?

"Sorry about the boots," Hammer said as she clumped into the room.

"I'm fine."

They all left the building together, and she looked toward her car. "I'll lead you out there."

"I'd prefer that you ride with us so you can show us where to stop."

I could have done that from my own car.

When she answered with a quick nod, they walked around to where the police cruisers were parked, and Hammer opened the front passenger door of one.

She climbed into the cruiser, and he shut the door firmly behind her.

Hammer drove. The two younger officers sat in the back section that was walled off with a wire cage.

As they left the city limits behind and drove into the foggy countryside, Hammer said, "The weather's pretty bad. How did you happen to be out here?"

"My aunt asked me to pick up some Christmas decorations from a woman on the island."

"Okay."

The conversation died, and Chelsea leaned forward, looking for the restaurant sign. When she finally saw it, she tried to gauge the spot where she'd seen the couple.

"Right there, I think," she murmured, pointing into the swamp.

Hammer pulled the cruiser to a stop and switched on the red and blue flashing lights, which cast an eerie glow on the bare winter landscape.

The three men got out and shone their flashlights on the ground, searching for signs of her earlier visit.

Hammer handed her a light, and she also shone it on the gravel. At first she saw nothing, and she was starting to think this might be the wrong place.

Then, to her vast relief, she spotted her own muddy footprints several yards beyond the car.

"Up there." She gestured with her flashlight beam.

"You get back in the cruiser and wait," the chief instructed. "We'll take care of this."

She shuddered as all three men drew their weapons. Then they started off in the direction she'd walked earlier. Thanks to their rubber boots, they kept going through the mucky area.

Once back in the police car she ignored good judgment that told her to lock the doors and keep the windows closed. Instead she leaned over and rolled the passenger window down so she could hear what was going on in the bog.

With the flashlight gripped tightly in her hand, she listened to sounds of feet splashing and watched lights bobbing in the moonlight. The beams moved away from her, sometimes jerking as the men struggled across the uneven ground.

Minutes ticked by as Chelsea waited, sure she was going to hear the cops come splashing back to her with disgusted expressions on their faces. Finally one of them shouted in the darkness.

"I've got a body."

Chapter Two

Chelsea gasped as the impact of the statement hit her like a blow to the chest. She had been prepared for something bad. But, to her own chagrin, she'd seen it in personal terms. She'd assumed that they weren't going to find anything real—and that once again she'd be ridiculed. Instead, someone was dead.

As she stared toward the swamp, a male figure came looming out of the fog. She dragged in a breath, holding it until she saw he was wearing a police officer's cap.

Seconds later, Draper was beside the cruiser.

"Who is it?" she asked.

"A woman."

"Did you find any identification?"

"This is a crime scene. We haven't searched her."

"Do you know what happened?"

"Not yet."

Before she could ask more questions, another beam

of light came out of the darkness. From the bulky shape that approached, she knew it was Hammer.

Draper moved deferentially out of the way so the chief could step up to the window of the cruiser.

"I understand you found a woman's body," Chelsea said.

"Yeah. I'm going to call in the state police. Since this is going to be a murder investigation."

As he pulled out his cell phone, he walked several yards up the road. She could hear him talking in a low voice, but she couldn't make out what he was saying.

"They'll be here soon," he said when he returned, then shifted his weight from one foot to the other. "I'd like to know if it was the female you saw."

Chelsea sucked in a sharp breath. "You mean you want me to look at the body?"

"Yeah."

"Is that standard police procedure?"

"That's *my* procedure," he growled, and she knew he wasn't pleased that she'd questioned his judgment.

"This way," Hammer said when she'd climbed out of the cruiser. "Best take my arm. It's slippery in the bog."

She didn't want to touch anyone right now. But she knew it was prudent to accept the chief's offer, particularly since her too-large boots were already making it hard to walk. So she grasped his arm and let him lead her into the bog, with Draper splashing along behind them.

Benson was waiting for them in the gloom. When they approached, he shone his flashlight onto a black shape on the ground. The beam illuminated a young woman lying on her side, her body half in and half out of a puddle of water. She was wearing a worn navy-blue or black coat and a shapeless gray dress that looked several sizes too big for her. Her eyes were closed and her dark hair was spread out in back of her as though she were still running through the bog, trying to get away from the man chasing her. A bloodstain spread out from below her body.

"I think that's the woman I saw," Chelsea whispered. "At least the hair and the coat look the same. I didn't get a good look at her face."

"Do you know who she is?"

"No." The wind had started to blow, and she had to clamp her jaw to keep her teeth from chattering.

"We'll want you to make a statement."

"I understand."

"And the state police will need to question you."

She looked back toward the road, sorry that she hadn't brought her own car. "Do I have to stay here?"

"When the state police get here, we'll take you back to the station where you can make your statement."

Chelsea gave up the battle to keep her teeth from chattering.

"Yeah, it's cold out here," Hammer agreed. "You can wait in the patrol car."

Of course, she wasn't only reacting to the cold. Seeing the woman up close had affected her deeply.

The victim looked so lost and alone out in the swamp. She'd been running from a man. Who was it? Her husband? Her lover? A guy she'd met in a bar?

No, she didn't look like the bar type. In fact, she looked strangely out of place in any context Chelsea could think of—except maybe a movie about displaced persons.

That was a strange thought. But she simply couldn't imagine this woman's life.

Chelsea and the cops started back across the muddy ground. When they reached the cruiser, she climbed into the passenger seat again. Draper slid behind the wheel, while Hammer went back to join Benson at the crime scene.

"Is it okay if I call my aunt?" Chelsea asked. "She's probably wondering why I'm not home yet."

"Go ahead."

She pulled out her cell phone—then remembered why she'd driven to the police station in the first place.

"Can I borrow your phone?" she asked Draper. "Mine's dead."

"Sure."

Aunt Sophie answered on the first ring. And her voice sounded worried.

"Chelsea, where are you? I was expecting you back an hour ago."

She'd wanted to reassure her aunt; now she

realized she should have planned what she was going to say. Certainly not that she'd led the cops to a dead body outside town.

"I ran into a little delay," she temporized.

"A traffic accident?" her aunt asked immediately.

"Nothing like that. I'll be home as soon as I can. Please don't worry about me. I'm fine."

She could have added that she was with the police. But she decided that would be going too far.

How long was she going to have to sit here before they drove her back to town? Damn. Why hadn't she insisted on taking her own car? Then she could go home and explain this to Aunt Sophie.

That thought didn't exactly calm her nerves. She didn't want to talk to her aunt about ghosts. She'd ignored the subject since coming back to Jenkins Cove. Now she was going to have to face the inevitable. And the worst part was that she hadn't chosen the time and place. This situation had been thrust upon her by circumstances.

MICHAEL BRYANT SWIVELED his desk chair toward the French doors and stretched out his long legs, crossing them at the ankles as he looked out the window of his comfortable office into the paved courtyard between the back of his two-story brick house and the detached garage. The large patio was surrounded by raised beds with small shrubs and perennial flowers that had gone underground for the winter.

Some people would have called it a charming little retreat. He called it low maintenance—the perfect balance in his life. An outdoor space he could enjoy when he wanted to get some fresh air, but at the same time, a garden he could maintain with very little effort.

Though born and raised in Chicago, he now lived in Washington, D.C., in the same house he'd rented a few years ago while working on a book about behind-the-scenes life in the White House. He liked the quiet, tree-lined street off Connecticut Avenue so much that when he'd gotten a chance to buy the property during a slump in the housing market, he'd jumped at it.

He shuffled through the stack of newspaper clippings on his desk, until he found the piece from the *Jenkins Cove Gazette,* a weekly paper published in a small town on the Eastern Shore of Maryland. His dark eyes narrowed, he reread the story that his clipping service had sent him.

Local Woman Leads Police to Mystery Body
By Helen Graham
The body of an unidentified woman was found three days ago in a bog along the highway between Jenkins Cove and Tilghman Island. Police got the tip from Jenkins Cove resident Chelsea Caldwell, who recently moved to town to help run the House of the Seven Gables Bed-

and-Breakfast. She led police to the body late in the evening.

Ms. Caldwell said she was returning from an evening trip when she saw a man and a woman struggling in a boggy area near the highway. When standing water prevented her from investigating, she alerted Police Chief Charles Hammer, who returned to the highway with her, accompanied by two patrol officers, Samuel Draper and Tommy Benson. After Ms. Caldwell showed them the location of the incident she had witnessed, the officers investigated and discovered the body of a woman about fifty feet from the road.

Upon finding the body, Chief Hammer turned the investigation over to the state police.

The unidentified victim is described as a young woman or a teenager, possibly a runaway.

Michael looked up from the text and slicked back the lock of dark hair that had fallen over his forehead while he'd been reading.

He'd wondered at first why the clipping service had sent him the article. Then he'd gotten to the next paragraph and figured it out.

Sources close to the police department note that when Ms. Caldwell made her report of the incident, she mentioned seeing a woman's body on the road prior to witnessing the assault. According to her statement, she got out of the car to look for the body, but it had vanished. A few hundred feet down the road, she witnessed the man and woman struggling in the bog.

Longtime local residents remember that as a child, Ms. Caldwell frequently spent summer vacations with her aunt, Sophie Caldwell, in Jenkins Cove. On one of those visits, she claimed to have seen a ghost near a playmate's house, but no one else could turn up any evidence of the visitation.

When asked if the long-ago ghost sighting might have any relationship to the current case, Ms. Caldwell refused to comment. Several witnesses report hearing Ms. Caldwell discuss the possibility that the victim on the road could have been a ghost.

Michael studied the picture that accompanied the article.

Chelsea Caldwell looked petite, with a face he'd call appealing. She had large light-colored eyes, a small upturned nose and chin-length wheat-colored hair. Not the sort of woman he'd think of as a liar. She looked too cute.

But Michael had learned that you couldn't make such assessments from a photograph. Sometimes it was even hard to do in person.

But from where he sat, the case was a perfect example of the kind of story he was looking for in his research. It was about a woman who needed to feel she was important, so she was making up ghost stories.

The body she'd found had obviously been real. But had she portrayed her part in the incident accurately? Why would she have said she'd seen a body on the road that conveniently vanished? To deflect attention from what had really happened?

He got up and stretched his long, lean frame, then strode to the French doors, picking up the basketball in the corner of the office on the way out.

After crossing the patio, he stepped into the alley, where he'd installed a hoop over the garage door. The air was nippy, but the alley was sheltered from the wind. He bounced the ball several times, then tossed it toward the hoop, made the shot and dribbled again.

Fifteen years ago, he'd been recruited out of high school by several colleges, but he'd turned down the basketball scholarships in favor of focusing on academics. He'd played for fun in college, and he still did some of his best thinking when he was on the court.

He thought about Chelsea Caldwell as he shot some more. A while later he went back inside, then sat at his desk again.

He'd started working on this ghost project several months ago, after Jeff Patterson had called him in a panic. Michael had grown up with Jeff, and they'd kept in touch over the years. Jeff worked for an investment firm, and he'd become alarmed when he'd found out several of his customers were taking financial advice from a medium—and losing a great deal of money in the process.

Michael had never believed in ghosts or anything else supernatural. In fact, Jeff's call had brought his own childhood experiences slamming back to him.

Apparently, he'd been so traumatized that he'd repressed some very unpleasant memories. After talking to Jeff, however, he'd recalled that his mom had often spent the grocery money on psychic readings while trying to contact his dead father.

Michael had gone to bed hungry and gone to school in clothing from the Salvation Army store because a series of psychics had gotten their hooks into his mother. Back then he'd vowed never to let himself be taken in by supernatural nonsense. His mom's mania had made him test everything—and believe in only what he could learn from his own senses.

Jeff's phone call had done more than bring back Michael's unpleasant memories. He wasn't a powerless kid anymore. He was a journalist with a national reputation. So he'd come back to Chicago, investigated the scam and exposed it in a major piece for a national magazine. The heady feeling of evening the score had made him want to do more. Now he was expanding his research into a book proposal.

His gaze came back to little Ms. Caldwell. She

intrigued him. He'd already dug into her background and found that she'd been selling paintings in Baltimore. Did she think her ghost stories would add to her cachet as an artist? Or had she tapped out artistically and was looking for another way to get some attention?

He wondered if the aunt was in on it. Were they using the ghost nonsense to get more customers for the B & B?

Well, finding out what made Ms. Caldwell tick wasn't going to be difficult. All he had to do was call up and make a reservation at the House of the Seven Gables.

He'd written exposés of the mob and helped get some wise guys put away in jail where they belonged. He'd accompanied an expedition down the Amazon and survived a very nasty spider bite in the process. He'd gotten in and out of a major African civil war without getting either of his arms lopped off.

Compared to that, investigating ghost stories on Maryland's Eastern Shore was going to be a piece of cake.

When he dialed the number of the B & B, a female voice answered, "House of the Seven Gables."

She sounded pleasant and professional—and just a little bit guarded. Odd for someone who made her living dealing with the public.

Was it her? The voice seemed too young to be the

aunt, but he wasn't going to ask her name, because that might tip her off that he had more than a casual interest in meeting the woman who had been written up in the paper.

Assuming that she wouldn't recognize his name, he said, "This is Michael Bryant. I'm hoping I can book a room for some time in the next few days."

"Have you looked at our Web site?"

"Yes."

"What room are you interested in?"

He hadn't made a thorough study of the photographs, so he said, "I don't really care. They all look nice. I'd just like to get away for a few days."

"The Preston Room is one of our best, and it's available starting December second."

"Just a moment." He looked at his calendar. December second was the day after tomorrow. Well, he was anxious to get this started, and the timing was perfect.

"That date works for me," he said, keeping his voice bland though he felt an unexpected jolt of excitement.

"The room has a private bath with a tub and shower combination. And it's in the front of the house, with a view of the harbor."

He leaned back in his chair, a smile flickering on his lips. "It sounds very appealing." Of course, he wasn't simply talking about the room, but he wasn't going to tell her that.

"Do you have any special dietary needs?" she asked.

She was efficient. For a moment he toyed with the idea of giving her something to worry about—then decided that telling her he needed a gluten-free diet would only make his stay at the inn less enjoyable.

So he answered, "No."

"How long will you be with us?"

"Let's say…a week."

"Fine," she said again. "We like to keep things quiet during the Christmas season, so you may be the only guest by the end of the week."

"That's perfect."

They transacted the rest of their business, and he hung up with the smile still on his face. If he was lucky, Chelsea Caldwell would end up as a chapter in his book—whether she liked it or not.

Chapter Three

Chelsea woke with a start, every muscle in her body instantly tense. Lying in the dark, she strained her ears. She'd thought she heard the sound of a voice whispering urgently to her.

Reaching for the bedside lamp, she pushed the switch, flooding the side of the bed with a pool of yellow light.

As she huddled under the covers, she scanned the room with her anxious gaze. There was no one in here. Had she dreamed someone was calling her?

She'd wakened like this more than once since the incident on the road.

The incident! That's what she'd been calling it, because she didn't want to think about murder. Or about ghosts.

Or discuss them, either. It wasn't like what that horrible newspaper article had said. She hadn't been blabbing to anyone. It was everyone else who was talking. But what was she supposed to do, write a letter to the editor in protest? That would only make things worse. Instead, she'd gone about her business and hoped the town would stop talking about her.

When she heard the sound of something clattering outside, she breathed out a sigh of relief. It wasn't a voice at all. It was real. But what was it?

Simply a raccoon trying to get into the trash cans? Or was somebody sneaking around the house?

"Stop jumping to the worst possible conclusions," she muttered. When she'd come back to Jenkins Cove, she'd convinced herself that life here was going to be normal and uneventful. Ever since she'd seen the woman lying in the road, nothing had felt normal.

If she'd been free to leave, she would have gone back to Baltimore. But she'd given up her apartment. And she'd made a commitment to staying and helping Aunt Sophie.

Now she hoped she wasn't making things worse for her aunt. Sometimes Chelsea would turn her head and catch Aunt Sophie staring at her. But then she would quickly look away.

Chelsea was pretty sure her aunt was worried about her. So she was doing her best to make it seem as though everything was okay. She could do that during the day, but at night she couldn't control where her unconscious mind took her. Apparently now she was translating sounds outside into nightmare whispers.

She swung her legs out of bed and tiptoed to the

window, looking out. A streetlight illuminated the side of the bed-and-breakfast. Down by the dock, another light shone on the small craft that were spending the winter in the sheltered harbor at the center of Jenkins Cove.

Fog wafted through the lights. As she stared at those spots of brightness, she thought she saw shapes swirling in the mist, shapes that took on human form.

No. That was ridiculous. It was just air moving.

She shivered, her eyes still fixed on the scene beyond the window as she imagined phantoms drifting through the town.

Damn!

Since her trip to Tilghman Island, ghosts had been on her mind. And she couldn't get them to go away.

She looked around the room. Well, the good news was that she wasn't seeing them in here. And she didn't want to. Which was why she hadn't gone near the third-floor room that Aunt Sophie called her "psychomanteum."

Chelsea made a sound low in her throat. Aunt Sophie had always been a little off-the-wall, but in the years since Chelsea had been away from Jenkins Cove, her aunt had let her eccentricities run wild. Now Chelsea had to cope with that, too.

She glanced at the clock on the nightstand. It was four in the morning. She should go back to bed, because she had to be up at seven to prepare breakfast for their guests. At the moment, they had three couples staying with them. One from Baltimore, one from Boston and one from Cleveland. The Cleveland couple were retired and traveling around the country, taking in holiday celebrations at various locations. The other four visitors were younger, and they had come to House of the Seven Gables for a weekend getaway.

Chelsea was about to climb back into bed when the same rattling sound made her stop in her tracks.

This time she thought it might be in the house.

Refusing to call the police, lest they think she'd gone hysterical, she pulled on her robe and grabbed the gun she'd started keeping in her bedside drawer. After slipping the weapon into the pocket of her robe, she scuffed her feet into bedroom slippers, stepped into the hall and started down the stairs, her hand in her pocket and her fingers wrapped around the butt of the gun.

The house was dark and quiet. All the guests were in their rooms, sleeping. The two weekend couples were leaving in the morning, and the maid would get the Preston Room ready for Michael Bryant, who was coming from Washington, D.C. He'd said he wanted to get away for a few days, but she'd wondered if he had more than that in mind.

Something in his voice had made her think he had a hidden agenda.

Silently, she admonished herself. Now she was

getting suspicious of Michael Bryant. Lately, it seemed, she didn't trust anyone.

But look what had happened with the cops. She'd made a report about the incident on the road, and because she'd wanted to be absolutely honest, she'd put in the part about the body she'd thought she'd seen on the road.

She was sorry she'd been so scrupulous, because evidently someone who had read the report had started talking about it. Was it Hammer? One of the patrolmen? Or a detective from the state police? Whoever it was, the breach of police confidentiality had led to talk about the ghost incident fifteen years ago.

She sighed. Since that article had come out in the local paper, she knew people were looking at her with curiosity in the grocery store and in the shops on Main Street. And she was sure they were talking about her behind her back.

Or was that just her own paranoia?

She had the number of that detective from the state police, Rand McClellan. Maybe she'd ask him if he knew something about the leak. Or maybe it was better to keep her mouth shut, hold her head up and ignore the town gossip.

She walked across the front hall, where the light had been left on to illuminate the steps.

She had reached the dining room and was just walking between the sideboard and the long Chippendale table when the kitchen door opened and a figure filled the doorway.

Chelsea started to draw the gun.

Then the man's shape registered. He was lean and stoop-shouldered, and she realized it was Mr. Thackerson, from Baltimore, wearing a T-shirt and jeans and bedroom slippers. He was coming out of the kitchen with a plate and a cup in his hand.

"Oh," he said. "Sorry to startle you."

"What…what are you doing down here?" she asked.

"I got hungry in the middle of the night, and I remembered that you had some delicious banana bread left over from yesterday's breakfast. It's one of my favorites. I hope you don't mind my helping myself to a slice—and some cranberry tea."

"No. That's fine," Chelsea allowed, seeing that he actually had two slices. Extra cake in the middle of the night wasn't really part of the deal, but she wasn't going to lecture him about it. She didn't want him bad-mouthing the House of the Seven Gables to his friends back in Baltimore. Instead, she stepped to the side, letting him pass her.

"I'll see you for breakfast in the morning," she said.

He mumbled an answer, his mouth already stuffed with Aunt Sophie's banana bread.

When he was gone, she leaned against the wall, breathing hard, thinking that she'd almost shot one of their guests.

She should get rid of the gun. But she couldn't do it. It was too much of a comfort to her.

After waiting a few minutes, she followed Mr. Thackerson back upstairs. In her room, she lay down and ordered herself to relax. She was going to look like hell if she didn't get some sleep. And instead of painting after lunch, she was going to have to take a nap.

She closed her eyes, thinking about all the things she had to do in the morning. Then she pushed them aside and focused on the painting that was half-finished in her studio upstairs. It was set in downtown Jenkins Cove, along Main Street.

Not one of her moody landscapes. It was for a holiday auction, so she'd deliberately painted a Christmas scene and set it at twilight so that she could show off her talent for bringing out the holiday lights.

As she let her mind picture the touches she was going to add tomorrow, she felt herself relax. Thinking about her work always soothed her. A good thing, because she needed to defuse her tension.

THE BRIGHT AFTERNOON SUN turned Jenkins Cove postcard perfect, Michael Bryant thought as he drove the length of Main Street, getting the lay of the land. This was definitely a tourist town. Very different from the gritty inner city where he'd grown up.

Most of the businesses that lined the street were decked out for the holiday season. Scattered among the shops were restaurants and real-estate offices—in case the tourists wanted to buy themselves a place in the land of pleasant living.

He circled the town square, where artificial icicles dangled from the roofline of a wooden gazebo, then passed two churches—one a Gothic stone and the other brick—on opposite sides of the street. They seemed to be in competition for the most elaborate crèche scene.

When he got to the outskirts of town, he turned right, heading down a residential street until the road stopped at the bank of what the locals probably called a creek. They used the word around here for bodies of water that he would have called rivers.

The creek was a surprise. He'd seen rivers and coves as he'd driven toward town, but he hadn't realized how much water hemmed in the community. Apparently you couldn't get very far without driving over a bridge—or into the water.

He turned around in the last driveway before the drink, then started back down Main Street. Consulting his computer-generated directions, he turned on Center Street, which dead-ended at Laurel. As he'd been instructed, he parked in the nearby public lot and wheeled his suitcase across the street toward the House of the Seven Gables.

The front garden was nicely tended, although winter obviously wasn't the best season to view it.

The house itself was a white clapboard building, three stories if you counted the dormer windows under the gabled roof. It looked as though it had been built in two or three stages.

Like every other building in town, it was adorned with Christmas decorations. The wreath on the front door was decorated with miniature duck decoys, and the garlands twined around the porch posts were studded with small sailboats and something red that he at first took for ribbons. Then he saw they were Maryland crabs.

Leaving his suitcase near the front entrance, he walked around to the water side and saw a long, two-story porch facing the harbor. Careful not to end up in the water, he turned and looked at the house. Shading his eyes for a better view, he counted at least five chimneys, hinting that the building had been constructed before central heating.

The inn had a prime waterfront location on the sheltered harbor at the center of town, directly across from a rambling seafood restaurant. Probably it was noisy in summer, but there weren't that many people operating boats at this time of year. For that, he was grateful.

A KNIT CAP COVERED the watcher's wiry brown hair. His jacket and pants were brown, too, giving him the appearance of a workman who had some off-season business at the dock area.

Yeah, he had business, all right. But it didn't have anything to do with repairing boats.

He was here to keep an eye on the House of the Seven Gables.

It was a boring job. But it paid well, and he wasn't complaining.

When the B & B guests were out, and the two ladies had gone out to get groceries, he'd used his lock picks and slipped inside the house to have a look around.

After helping himself to one of Aunt Sophie's chocolate-chip brownies, he'd looked at the guest book and snooped in some of the rooms. Back in the kitchen, he'd taken a long look at the step stool pulled up at the side of the cooking island.

He'd seen Chelsea climb up on it to get something from a high cabinet. Maybe if he loosened the leg a little bit, she'd fall and break her neck. He'd be rid of one problem.

Now he leaned forward, zeroing in on the tall, dark-haired man prowling around the house. From his perusal of the guest book in the office, he suspected it was Michael Bryant, who was scheduled to arrive that afternoon. His build was athletic, and he was wearing dress slacks and an expensive V-neck sweater over a dress shirt. Not the grubby attire of some of the tourists who showed up in town.

The watcher noted the man was prowling around.

Not your typical guest behavior. But he'd already looked up Bryant on the Web, using the computer at the library.

Apparently, the guy was an investigative reporter. So what was he investigating?

Murder in Jenkins Cove?

That was a good bet. Bryant definitely didn't look as though he was just here on vacation. At least, most people who came to a B & B didn't start by poking around the outside property. They introduced themselves first and got settled in their rooms—then went exploring.

Or maybe he was interested in ghost stories.

The watcher snorted. Well, he'd come to the right place, if town gossip was any indication.

The porch door opened, and Chelsea Caldwell stepped out, dressed in jeans and a cable-knit sweater. After watching her for days, he knew she'd be casually dressed, even when she was expecting guests.

He liked the way she filled out the jeans. Too bad the sweater covered her curves.

She stood for a moment with her hands on her hips, observing the nosy guy. Then she dropped her arms to her sides, squared her shoulders and came down the steps.

"Can I help you?" she called out in a loud voice.

As soon as Mr. Bryant and Chelsea went inside, he was going to make a report on this meeting.

MICHAEL TURNED AROUND and saw a woman coming down the steps. Petite, blond, with blue eyes and an upturned nose, she was immediately recognizable.

Chelsea Caldwell in the flesh.

"Can I help you?" she asked.

To his annoyance, he felt an instant zing of attraction. He hadn't come down here to start anything with her. He'd come to find out why she'd made up the ghost stories.

He shoved his hands into his pockets. "I'm Michael Bryant. I've booked a room here."

"Chelsea Caldwell," she answered. "I believe we spoke over the phone. I saw you looking around, and I wondered if you were thinking about staying here."

"I wanted to get an impression of the exterior before I came inside," he answered, thinking that the explanation sounded stuffy. And maybe defensive. That wasn't the way he wanted to start off, but now he was stuck with it.

"Well, I'll be waiting for you in the office. It's to the left of the front door."

"I'll come with you."

He followed her along a path made of some kind of white rocks that crunched under his feet. "This some kind of special gravel?"

"Oyster shells."

"Oh." Yeah, that made sense in an area where half the people made their living from the water.

When they came around to the front of the house,

he reached for the handle of the suitcase at the same time Chelsea did, and their hands collided with a little jolt of electricity. They both drew back quickly and said "Sorry" at the same time.

"Electricity in the air," she murmured.

"Yes." Folding down the handle, he carried the bag up the steps to the front porch, then into a square front hall.

As soon as he stepped inside, delicious aromas wrapped themselves around him, and he took an appreciative breath.

Chelsea was watching him. "Aunt Sophie loves to bake. If you don't watch out, you'll gain weight while you're here."

"Warning taken."

Chelsea led the way past what looked like genuine antique furnishings to the office.

"I'm sure you'll like Jenkins Cove," she said. "What brings you here?"

"I just wanted to get away and enjoy the small-town holiday atmosphere," he answered, thinking that she wasn't what he'd expected at all. After reading the article, he'd wondered if she was involved in the murder. In person, he was having trouble picturing her in that role. Then he reminded himself sharply that he'd just met her, and that he had no basis to form an impression.

Moreover, the instant attraction he'd felt was dangerous.

He realized she was speaking again. "You're welcome to watch television or visit with the other guests in the living room. We also have a collection of DVDs that you can use with the television in your room."

"I should have asked, do the rooms have Internet access?"

"We've got a wireless network."

"Great," he said, meaning it. He'd be able to keep up his research while he was here.

"Breakfast is usually between eight and nine-thirty," she told him. "If you want to eat earlier, we can make special arrangements." She consulted a sheet of paper. "You said you didn't have any dietary restrictions."

"That's right."

"That makes it easy." She started toward the door and must have seen that they were going to touch again if she tried to get past him.

Obediently, he stepped out of the way.

"The Preston Room is down here. You'll have a nice view of the water."

As they stepped into the living room, a plump woman wearing a dark skirt and blouse covered by a long white apron came bustling through a doorway. Her hair was pulled back in a bun, and her lined face was wreathed in smiles. It was obvious that she was related to Chelsea. The shape of her face was the same, and her gray hair still had some traces of gold.

"You must be Michael Bryant," she said.

"And you must be the woman who makes this house smell like a five-star bakery."

She flushed. "I'm Sophie Caldwell, and you've already met my niece, Chelsea."

"Yes."

"We serve tea and cookies and wine and cheese in the parlor in the afternoon at five. You're welcome to join us."

"Thank you."

"So, what do you do for a living?" she asked, taking him aback with the bluntness of the question.

"I'm a writer."

"Oh, that's so interesting. You know James Michener lived in the area when he was writing *Chesapeake*."

"Yes."

"And you'll find the books of a number of local writers in the shops on Main Street. Are you writing a novel?"

"Yes," he said. He had an idea for a novel that he was toying with. But that wasn't what he was working on now, of course.

"Does Jenkins Cove have a ghost tour?" he asked.

He saw Chelsea stiffen. But her aunt's expression turned apologetic. "I'm sorry. The merchants' association has talked about it, but we never got around to doing anything about it."

"So are you saying there are ghosts in town?" he asked.

"There are ghosts in every town," Sophie answered serenely. "And, of course, Jenkins Cove has had its share of murders over the years." She lowered her voice as she said the last bit.

She seemed as though she was about to add something else, but her niece's narrow-eyed look made her close her mouth.

"I have some things to do in the kitchen," Chelsea said in a strained voice. "Aunt Sophie, would you mind showing Mr. Bryant to his room?"

"I'll be glad to. Come this way. You're on the first floor."

Chelsea hurried off, and the older woman led him down a hall to the Preston Room, which featured a bed with a blue and gold canopy that matched the drapes tied back over white-painted plantation shutters.

"Your niece seemed to get upset when I mentioned ghost tours," he commented.

"She had a bad experience recently."

"What happened?" he asked innocently.

She gave him a direct look, and he had the fleeting feeling that she'd seen through his ruse. But instead of calling him on his motivation, she said, "If she wants to tell you about it, she will."

She left him alone, and he sat in the comfortable

chair by the window, flipping through the brochures Chelsea had given him.

He'd been in his room for about an hour when he heard voices down the hall. Glancing at his watch, he saw that it was about time for the wine and cheese hour.

When he walked into the front hall, he saw a thin, sallow-skinned woman standing by the stairs with Aunt Sophie, looking uncertain.

"There's nothing to be nervous about, dear," Aunt Sophie was saying.

"I've never done anything like this before," the woman said softly.

"Well, you're very brave to take this step. It's always a big decision to try and reach across the great divide to a loved one."

Michael stared from Sophie to the older woman. "Contacting the dead?" he said, hearing the rough quality of his own voice.

"Why, yes."

"You have people coming here for séances?" he asked, struggling not to make his voice sound accusing.

Aunt Sophie laughed. "Séances? No, no. They can be faked, of course. But I have built a psychomanteum in the attic."

"A psychomanteum?" he asked, as he rolled the pretentious-sounding word around in his mouth. "What's that?"

She smiled serenely. "You look alarmed. But it's nothing to worry about. It's just a room where the dead can contact the living—if they so choose."

Chapter Four

From the corner of his eye, Michael saw that Chelsea had stepped into the hall and gone stock-still when she realized that the subject had turned to ghosts—again.

Funny how they kept coming up.

"That sounds very interesting. I'd like to hear about this psychomanteum," he said, looking from niece to aunt.

Sophie gave him a bright smile. "I read about it on the Web. You can pick up so much information on the Web, don't you know? I started doing research on psychic phenomena after…" She glanced at Chelsea and stopped short.

"After what?" Michael prompted, pretty sure what she had stopped herself from saying. After Chelsea had said she'd seen a ghost. Of course the question was—which time? Fifteen years ago or last week?

Ignoring the question, the older woman went on. "I found a Web site that told all about it. It's a very ancient concept. Long ago, people might go into the forest, kneel down by a pool of water and peer into it as they asked the spirit of a dead relative to come to them. Today we're more likely to use a darkened room, hung with heavy curtains. My psychomanteum has a chair and a mirror, and candles for light. You sit in the chair, stare into the mirror and invite a spirit to come to you."

Michael wanted to tell her she was out of her mind. Either that or she'd found some way to make the psychomanteum pay big-time. Instead he settled for a noncommittal "I see," before turning toward Chelsea. "Have you ever tried it?"

"No!" she said sharply, then looked at her aunt. "And I don't intend to."

"It might help you," Sophie said softly, and Michael waited to see what Chelsea would say.

"I don't need that kind of help," she answered, and Michael gathered that he'd stepped into the middle of an old argument.

Chelsea looked from her aunt to Michael, then seemed to realize that there was a fourth person in the room.

"Mrs....Albright?"

"Yes, dear," her aunt answered. "Mrs. Albright and I were talking in church about her dear departed husband, Norbert. She said she wished she could speak to him again, and I suggested she try the psychomanteum."

Chelsea answered with a tight nod.

"How much do you charge to use the psychomanteum?" Michael asked Sophie.

She looked startled. "Why, nothing. It's just…" She shrugged. "Just something I do for the community." Turning to Mrs. Albright, she said, "I'll take you up, dear, and get you settled." Then she asked her niece, "Can you get out the wine and cheese?"

"Yes."

"And don't forget those brownies and lemon bars I made this afternoon. I'll be down in a few minutes."

Sophie and her guest started up the stairs.

When the two women had reached the second floor and started down the hall, Michael leaned toward Chelsea. "Do you believe that? That people can contact the dead?"

"I don't know."

"Have you ever done it?"

"Have you?" she shot back.

"No."

"At least you're sure of what you believe."

"What's that supposed to mean?"

Instead of answering, she turned on her heel and headed for the dining room, where she exited through a door at the far end of the room.

Michael thought about waiting for her in the living room, since it might not be appropriate for the guests to go into the working part of the B & B.

The heck with it. He followed her through the doorway and found himself in the kitchen.

Chelsea was just setting wineglasses on a silver tray when the back door of the house opened, and a nattily dressed man in his midthirties walked in. He was of medium height with medium brown hair carefully combed to the side.

Chelsea's head jerked up. "Ned, what are you doing here?"

"Have you talked to your aunt about my offer?" He thrust his hands into the pockets of his gray slacks.

"No. And I'm not going to."

"The market could go down."

"That won't make any difference to Aunt Sophie. She's not interested in selling."

Michael cleared his throat. "Am I interrupting something? I was in a hurry to get here, so I didn't stop for lunch on the way down from D.C., and I was hoping for a head start on the wine and cheese."

"Of course," Chelsea answered, apparently glad that he was in the kitchen. She went to the refrigerator and took out a bottle of white Chablis, along with a tray that held crackers and small slices of cheese. "White or red wine?" she asked.

The brown-haired man gave Michael an annoyed look.

He could have cut the tension in Chelsea's voice with one of the knives in the rack under the window. "Red."

Picking up a glass she'd set on the tray, she poured from a bottle of Merlot. As she handed Michael the glass, she said, "Ned just stopped by for his weekly reminder that the House of the Seven Gables is sitting on prime town land and Aunt Sophie could make a fortune if she sold it to a developer."

The other man kept his expression neutral.

"But he's not going to get Aunt Sophie to sell," Chelsea finished.

"I'd like to talk to her," he said.

"She's busy."

He might have kept pressing his case. Instead he held up his hands, palms out. "Okay, another time," he answered with an edge in his voice. Then he exited the kitchen.

Michael watched him disappear down the walk. "He's pushy."

"Ned Perry never learned how to take no for an answer. With some people, it works. But Aunt Sophie loves this place. She'll never sell while she's still alive."

"If she sold, wouldn't she make enough to retire in luxury?"

Chelsea turned to him, her face set in firm lines. "She doesn't want to retire. That's why I came back to Jenkins Cove—to help her take care of this place." She blinked. "I'm sorry. You don't want to hear about our business."

"Actually, I do. I find that little drama very interesting."

"Well, the drama is over." She picked up the

tray of cheese. "You can help me carry the wine and glasses."

"Sure."

When they returned to the living room, two more guests were seated on the sofa. Both gray-haired and slightly overweight, they were eating from the plate of cookies on the coffee table. Chelsea set down the tray of cheese, and Michael put the wine and glasses beside it. She took a straight chair by the door, leaving an easy chair for him.

"I'm Michael Bryant," he said.

"Ted Alexander."

"And Betty Alexander," the woman added. "We've been here for a few days. You'll love Jenkins Cove and the House of the Seven Gables."

Just as Michael sat down, Aunt Sophie joined them. "Well, it's nice to see you all."

"Where's Mrs. Albright?" Michael asked.

"She's still upstairs."

"She came to use the psychomanteum," Michael said helpfully.

Chelsea gave him a dark look, but Betty Alexander smiled broadly. "Oh yes. The ghost room upstairs. Ted won't have anything to do with it, but I tried it, hoping to have a little adventure. Unfortunately, nothing happened. I guess there were no spirits that wanted to contact me."

Ted gave his wife an indulgent smile. "It's a bunch of hooey, you know. But harmless."

"Now, now," Sophie answered. "Don't dismiss it out of hand. It might work for you—if you believed." She was about to say something else when the front door opened, and a tall, rangy man wearing dark slacks and a rumpled sports coat walked in.

Another guest? Come just in time for the afternoon snack.

"Sorry to interrupt," he said, looking around at the group seated in the living room.

"Oh, Detective McClellan," Aunt Sophie answered. "How nice to see you. Would you like a cookie or some wine and cheese?"

"No, thanks, ma'am. I came to talk to Ms. Caldwell," he said, glancing at the niece.

"Yes, right." She stood up and looked around at the faces turned in her direction. "Let's go into the den."

The cop nodded.

When he and Chelsea had left the room, Michael asked, "That was a police detective?"

Mrs. Alexander leaned forward. "She saw a murder in the swamp. Along the highway, you know."

"No!" Michael answered, feigning ignorance and surprise.

"Yes. And she saw a ghost, too."

"You don't know that," Mr. Alexander interjected. "I think she was just scared and overreacting, you know. Anyway, the local cops called in the state police."

Michael inclined his head toward the hallway. "Is that where he's from?"

"Yes," Sophie answered. She sighed. "Chelsea doesn't like to talk about what happened. It's too bad that ghost story got around town."

"You mean the ghost she saw when she was a little girl?" Betty Alexander asked.

"Both," her husband said. "The ghost she saw when she was a little girl and the one she saw on the road before she spotted the man and woman struggling in the swamp."

Michael sat back and listened. He hadn't picked up any new facts about the case. But he had found out something interesting. Apparently everyone in town knew about the two incidents. And they were willing to talk to tourists about it.

As he'd assumed, Chelsea had turned herself into a local celebrity.

DETECTIVE RAND MCCLELLAN of the state police waited while Chelsea Caldwell closed the door to the den, then turned toward him, a set look on her face.

He'd first interviewed her at the Jenkins Cove Police Station. The witness who discovered a body was always one of the murder suspects. And he'd investigated her pretty thoroughly. He was almost certain that she wasn't involved in the murder, although he still had to keep that option open.

He was here now to show her some pictures of

known criminals. "Could you look at some photos and tell me if any of the men might be the man you saw attacking the woman?"

He laid a stack of photos on the table, and she paged through them, stopping several times.

When she finally looked up, she shook her head. "I don't think it's any of them. Who are they?"

"Men who were involved in crimes against women in various locations in Maryland."

"I'm sorry I can't help you. It was pretty dark that night. And the man was…too far away for me to get a good look at him."

"But you're sure it was none of these guys."

"I can't be absolutely sure. But I don't think so."

"We may have some more pictures later."

As he put the photos back into a folder, she cleared her throat.

"Yes?" he asked.

"You saw the newspaper story about the murder?"

"Yes."

"Do you happen to know who read my police report and gave the information to the newspapers?" she asked. Perhaps the question came out more sharply than she'd intended, because a flush came into her cheeks.

"Sorry. Yeah, I did notice that. But a lot of people had access to the report. I'd say it was from the Jenkins Cove PD, but I know that would sound self-serving."

She sighed. "I think it's more likely them than the

state police. My guess is that one of the patrol officers wanted to make himself look like a big shot."

Rand made a disgusted sound. "Yeah. They were both young. I can talk to Chief Hammer about making sure his men maintain the confidentiality of police information."

He watched her work through the implications.

Apparently, her thoughts were running along the same track. "I hope you won't tell him you spoke to me about it."

"Of course not."

Changing the subject, she asked, "Are you making any progress in finding out who the dead woman is?"

He could tell her that he couldn't give out information about the investigation. Instead, he said, "We think she might be a runaway from Baltimore or some other part of the country."

As he spoke, he watched her closely. Maybe she wasn't involved in the murder, but she was certainly on edge.

"Because she matches the description of a missing person?" Chelsea asked.

"No, because we simply don't know *who* she is. One couple thought it might be their daughter and came down here to look at the body. But it wasn't her."

"I'm glad, for their sake," Chelsea answered softly. "You'll tell me if you find out her name?"

"Yes." He hesitated for a moment, then said, "I'd better be going."

"Was there something you wanted to tell me?"

"No," he denied, then opened the door of the den. "I can let myself out. You go back to your guests."

Rand walked out the front door, closing it behind him. He'd toyed with the idea of getting Ms. Caldwell's reaction to a piece of information from the autopsy. But he'd decided that there were enough leaks in the case.

The interview had given him another opportunity to observe her. She'd told a story about a ghost that would have most cops shaking their heads. Rand, however, had found out a couple of years ago that there could be more to a case than you could verify through your own senses or the usual police work. When he'd been investigating an explosion and multiple murders at the Cranebrook Labs in St. Stephens, some of the facts simply hadn't added up. In fact, he'd been sure the wrong guy—Gage Darnell—had murdered his partner, until Gage had convinced Rand that he was the fall guy, not the perp.

This case had some similar aspects. Was someone setting up Chelsea Caldwell? Or was she an innocent bystander who'd been at the wrong place at the wrong time?

To Chelsea's disgust, when she returned to the living room, the group was still taking about ghosts. Aunt Sophie was telling a story that Chelsea had heard dozens of times before—about a boat that had come sailing into the Jenkins Cove Harbor and bumped up against the dock.

"People thought they saw a young man on the deck," Sophie whispered. "Working the sails and manning the tiller. But when they investigated, the only person they'd found on the boat was downstairs in the main cabin."

She looked around, making her audience wait for the punch line. "It was a very sick young woman who claimed that she and her husband had been out sailing. Both of them had gotten food poisoning, and he put her to bed, then came up to sail the boat into port. The woman was taken right to the hospital, where she recovered. Nobody ever found a trace of the man, and a lot of people think his ghost sailed the boat to Jenkins Cove as his last loving act before crossing over."

The Alexanders were listening wide-eyed. Michael Bryant was sitting back in his chair with a skeptical look plastered on his face. When he saw Chelsea standing in the doorway, he said, "What do you think?"

"I think he sailed the boat into the harbor and then tumbled overboard."

"Did they ever find his body?"

"Not that I know of."

"Because it wasn't there. It was somewhere out in the bay," Aunt Sophie said.

Chelsea shrugged. She looked as though she was

about to say something, when a noise in the hall made her turn. It was Mrs. Albright.

Aunt Sophie jumped up. "Did you speak to your husband?" she asked.

Mrs. Albright's eyes brimmed. "No."

"I'm so sorry. But we can't always count on the spirits being available," Aunt Sophie said. She got up and the two women walked across the hall, talking in low tones. When they stepped outside, Michael lost sight of them.

"This is all so fascinating," Mrs. Alexander said.

"It's good party conversation," her husband answered.

Chelsea gestured stiffly toward the trays on the table. "Feel free to help yourselves. I'll be back later for the trays." She looked at Michael. "We lock the door in the evenings, so please take the key when you go out." Addressing the room in general, she added, "I'll see you all at breakfast. Can you give me some idea when you'd like to eat?"

"Eight-thirty," Mrs. Alexander said. "We'd like to get an early start in the morning."

"I'd like to sleep in. So nine would be good," Michael said, figuring he could avoid eating most of the meal with the couple, since he didn't particularly like them.

Mrs. Alexander looked disappointed. Her husband gave him a little shrug.

It was already getting dark as Michael turned and

walked down the hall, thinking he should take another look at the list of area restaurants he'd gotten when he checked in.

But his mind was on Chelsea. Initially he'd thought she was a woman who wanted everyone to marvel at the fact that she had seen two ghosts. To the contrary, however, she seemed to want to avoid the subject.

That led him back to his theory that she was somehow involved in the murder. And perhaps the ghost business was a smoke screen…

He'd like to talk to her about it some more. But he'd found out in the past few hours that she wouldn't welcome the topic.

Well, maybe he could start with something else and work his way back to the ghosts. That might be the right approach.

Or maybe he should give up the idea of including her in his book.

He blinked, wondering where that wayward thought had come from. He'd come all the way down here to corner her, and he wasn't going to let her put him off. He wanted to find out what made her tick. For professional *and* personal reasons.

He brought himself up short. Personal reasons had no place in his plans. At least not where Chelsea Caldwell was concerned.

CHELSEA COULD NOT STOP thinking of Michael Bryant. Not as a guest. As a man. A very handsome man.

Carrying the tray of glasses to the kitchen, she stopped short, nearly spilling the crystal, as a realization hit her with a jolt.

She was attracted to him. Strongly attracted.

And that was too bad, because she couldn't shake the feeling that he wasn't being entirely honest with her and Aunt Sophie.

Maybe the mistrust had started right at the beginning—when she'd seen him prowling around the outside of the house before stopping in the office to tell them he had arrived.

She filled the sink with soap and water, then began to wash the wineglasses, since she didn't trust stemware in the dishwasher.

As she worked, the light by the kitchen door gave a pop and went out.

"Damn," she muttered.

At this time in the evening, she needed all the light she could get if she was going to wash Mrs. Alexander's lipstick off the wineglass. So she got another bulb from the pantry, then carried over the kitchen stool that she kept under the edge of the island.

The stool seemed a little more shaky than usual, but she was in a hurry, so she climbed up and started to unscrew the shade.

MICHAEL TUCKED THE restaurant brochures into his back pocket and walked back toward the public areas of the house. He had a legitimate reason to talk to Chelsea now—if he could find her.

A couple of lamps burned in the living room, but the trays of cheese and wine had been cleared away.

"Chelsea?"

When she didn't answer, he listened for a moment and thought he heard a noise down the hall.

Hurrying through the dining room, he pushed open the swinging door into the kitchen and heard a scrabbling sound—and a gasp.

Chapter Five

Michael's heart leaped into his throat as he sprang through the door. He was in time to see a kitchen stool toppling over, and hear a crash as Chelsea hurtled toward the floor.

He caught her before she landed, pulling her body tightly against his. His heart was pounding like a tom-tom in his chest as he tightened his hold on her, struggling to keep them both from falling over.

Her hands flew over his back, then settled on his shoulders. As the two of them regained their balance, he waited for her to push him away, but she still clung to him.

He muttered a curse under his breath, then added, "I'm so sorry."

He'd come charging into the kitchen like a bull chasing a red flag, and apparently he'd knocked Chelsea off the stool when she was changing a light-bulb.

Now he was holding her in his arms. She felt

warm and feminine in his embrace. And more fragile than he would have imagined.

"Are you all right?" he asked, the question coming out low and gritty.

"Yes."

Now was the time to turn her loose. His brain registered that fact, but his arms simply wouldn't drop away from her body.

He felt her move, but it was only to raise her face to his. There he saw her questioning look and a very appealing flush spread across her cheeks.

He focused on her lips, then raised his gaze to her eyes. Time stretched, long enough for an eternity of silent messages to pass between them. Somewhere in his mind, he knew none of this should be happening. He shouldn't be holding her—for so many reasons.

He had come here because…

At this moment, the reason didn't matter. The only thing his brain had room for was that she was standing in his embrace.

That was reality. Their reality.

His gaze switched to her mouth again. Her lips were parted now, her breath shallow. Slowly, giving her a chance to pull away, he lowered his head, and his mouth touched down on hers.

Had he meant to be gentle? Had he meant to comfort her?

Those were his intentions. And that was the way the kiss started. She was passive for a moment.

Maybe she was even shocked. But then he felt her respond to him. The returned pressure of her lips against his fueled a hot, frantic jolt inside him— a jolt that reverberated between them and at the same time wrapped itself around them like a protective shield.

A cannon could have gone off beside the house, and the explosion wouldn't have made them move away from each other.

He heard a sound well up in her throat. Or perhaps it was from his throat. He couldn't be sure.

He felt her hands roving restlessly over his back, his shoulders, and he found he was doing the same thing to her.

They clung together, rocking slightly in the middle of the room as the kiss turned more urgent, more hungry.

The taste and feel of Chelsea Caldwell were the only reality in his universe. Well, that and the pounding arousal of his own body that swept away all thoughts but one.

He wanted her with an urgency that he had never felt before.

His mouth moved over hers, feasting on her. She kissed him with the same hunger. When she opened her lips, he accepted the invitation, his tongue sliding along the rigid line of her teeth, then beyond.

She met the invasion eagerly, fueling his need for more. With deliberate purpose, he eased far enough away to slide one hand between them so that he could gently cup her breast and stroke his fingers over the tip.

It had turned hard, abrading his fingers through her blouse. Thank the Lord she had taken off the sweater so that the bulky garment didn't get in his way.

The small sounds she made in her throat sent sparks along his nerve endings. Like the electric shock of the first time he'd touched her. That must have been a promise of things to come.

"Chelsea."

She answered with his name.

He took a step back, taking her with him, thinking that he would brace his hips against the kitchen counter so that he could equalize their heights and bring her center against his erection.

But as he moved his foot, something crunched under his heel.

It sounded like broken glass.

She went rigid in his arms.

His eyes blinked open and he saw a look of panic bloom on her face.

"What are you doing?" she gasped.

"You mean what are *we* doing?" he heard himself correct her, maybe because he was feeling defensive about his own impulsive behavior.

He wanted to look away, but he kept his gaze steady. "Whatever it was, there were two people involved."

She had the grace not to challenge him on that.

"Yes," she whispered, and flushed again, only this time he knew it was from embarrassment, not passion.

His head was spinning as he scrambled to rearrange his thinking.

He'd come to Jenkins Cove to investigate the ghost stories Chelsea Caldwell was spreading around town to make herself important. Or to obscure something more sinister.

Since he'd arrived, she'd acted as if she wished all the fuss would die down. Then he'd burst through the kitchen door and knocked her down—and caught her in his arms. And she'd stayed there.

It had been an accident, for all the good that did him.

She was staring at him with a look of distress in her eyes—a look far different from her earlier expression.

"I'm sorry," he said. The words sounded lame, even to his own ears.

"This is crazy."

"I know."

"We can't do this."

"I know," he said again.

She backed away and crunched on glass again.

He looked down to make sure that she wasn't wearing sandals or something else dangerous. "Let me help you clean that up."

"I can do it."

He started to protest, but she cut him off. "Please leave."

He started to comply. Then he saw the stool lying on its side. One of the legs was bent at a strange angle. He walked over and picked it up. "This is broken."

"What?"

"The stool broke when it fell."

"But it only fell on its side." She inspected the leg, looking perplexed.

"You'd better get rid of it."

"I don't need your advice."

"Right. Sorry." He backed away. He could have argued that they needed to talk about what had happened. But he couldn't exactly imagine the conversation, and he had the good sense to step back through the door.

He walked to his room and grabbed his jacket, then left the B & B, heading for Main Street. He didn't care what restaurant he went to now; he just needed to get out of the house.

Now that the sun had set, the air had turned nippy, and the cold helped clear his head. But he still didn't know what had happened to him.

Chelsea Caldwell was a woman he didn't want to like. A woman he was investigating because he thought she was into some kind of scam. But doubts about his judgment kept cropping up in his mind. And as soon as he'd folded her into his arms, everything had changed.

He'd felt something simmering between them

from the first moment they'd met. It had flashed into a rolling boil with alarming speed.

He considered going back to the B & B, grabbing his suitcase and leaving. For a whole lot of reasons. Did he really want to prove she was a fraud?

He swore under his breath. A few hours ago he'd been absolutely sure of his purpose. Now, however, he realized this research trip to Jenkins Cove wasn't exactly turning out the way he'd expected.

That was the way his profession worked, he reminded himself. You came in with certain assumptions, and you had to be prepared to change them if the facts warranted.

As he walked down Center Street, past an old warehouse that stood dark and hulking in the night, something strange happened. He came to a place where the atmosphere was suddenly colder than it had been just moments before. He raised his head and looked around, expecting to see that the wind had picked up and was blowing the branches of the trees around. But the air was still as a pond that was covered with a sheet of ice.

Then a prickling sensation at the back of his neck made him whirl around to find out who was watching him.

Every instinct told him that someone was there. When his eyes probed the shadows, he saw nothing. Yet the feeling of being watched only grew stronger. And the air seemed to darken or flicker.

"Who's there?" he called out, taking a step toward the spot where it seemed he might have seen some movement in the darkness.

"Come out and show yourself."

No one answered, and he stood on someone's lawn for several moments, frustration bubbling inside him.

He prided himself on being a rational man. But at this moment, he felt that something was happening totally outside his control. He didn't feel the wind blowing, but he heard something. A high-pitched whispering that grated on his ears and his nerve endings.

He tried to take a step forward, but he felt as if he'd hit an invisible barrier that held him in place.

He clenched his teeth, thinking this was the strangest experience he had ever had. It was getting weirder by the heartbeat.

Along with the strange sound, he thought he heard words, and strained to hear them. He couldn't bring the syllables into focus so that they made any sense.

It was as though someone was speaking to him over a radio frequency, but he wasn't equipped to bring in the signal.

Or, to put it another way, he might have said that a phantom from the invisible world had invaded this stretch of Center Street. A phantom that was here to give Michael Bryant a warning, or an urgent message that he wasn't able to capture.

A warning or a message from a phantom?

He shook his head, dismissing the outlandish notion, yet at the same time feeling the pounding of his own heart.

Apparently, he was so off balance from his encounter with Chelsea that he was seeing ghosts in the bushes and hearing their voices in the air.

"No."

As he spoke, reality twisted again. The air grew a few degrees warmer, and suddenly he found that nothing was holding him in place. He could walk forward.

No, nothing had been *holding* him in the first place. Nothing besides the inability to make his own muscles move.

Still, when he found out that he was free, he began walking rapidly toward the Christmas lights and the holiday crowds on Main Street. When he realized he was practically running, he made an effort to slow down, cursing under his breath.

Was he losing it? First that kiss in the kitchen, and now this.

Whatever this was.

CHELSEA SWEPT THE BROKEN lightbulb into a dustpan. Then she wet some paper towels and picked up the tiny pieces of glass that she couldn't see, working slowly and methodically.

She'd once gotten a piece of glass in her bare foot,

and it had been painful—worse than a wooden splinter. She didn't want to repeat that experience.

The remembered pain wasn't the only reason she was concentrating so fiercely. She wanted to focus on the job at hand—not what had happened between herself and Michael Bryant.

He'd knocked her off the stool when he'd come into the kitchen. Then he'd caught her before she'd hit the floor.

So far, so good.

The rest of it was what she couldn't wrap her head around. She'd ended up in his arms, and she'd stayed there. The embrace had turned into a kiss.

He'd brought his hand up between them and cupped her breast, rubbed his fingers across her nipple. She should have stopped him. Truth to tell, she hadn't wanted him to stop.

It was only when his foot had crunched on the glass that she'd come to her senses.

What in the name of God was wrong with her? After the first ghost incident, she'd been careful not to let people know the real Chelsea Caldwell until she was sure it was safe. That had cut down on her social life because she came across as guarded in personal relationships. After that she'd withdrawn even further into her work.

That was one reason the B & B was good for her. It forced her to interact with people. She enjoyed it, maybe because she knew the guests would be leaving in a few days and she didn't have to keep up a relationship with them.

Was that what she'd done with Michael Bryant? Subconsciously decided he was "safe"?

Surely not because she trusted him.

Or had she responded on a more base, primal level? He was a handsome, sexy man, and she was a healthy young woman. Well, she'd have to be careful not to let it happen again. And not to be alone with him.

Really, she'd like to tell him to find another B & B in Jenkins Cove. She was even willing to help him do it. But she couldn't let her personal feelings get in the way of Aunt Sophie's business.

After finishing with the glass, she walked over to the stool and looked at the leg. Michael was right. She'd better get rid of it.

The stool had been fine the last time she'd used it, she recalled. What had happened? Had a ghost come into the B & B and broken it?

She tried to laugh, but the sound only grated in her ears.

MICHAEL THOUGHT ABOUT GOING into the first restaurant he came to, but he refused to acknowledge that he was uncomfortable out in the open. He kept walking down the main street of the town. The shops were closed, but all of them were decked out in their holiday best, many with waterman themes. He even saw some ornaments made out of oyster shells or fishermen's nets.

He walked for several blocks until the commercial establishments began to thin out. There was only one more place up ahead of him.

It was called the Duck Blind, and when he walked inside, he found it was an informal bar and restaurant with wood-paneled walls, a plank floor and tables lit by fake stained-glass chandeliers.

It seemed so familiar, so normal after his strange experience on Center Street. He'd started to question his own sanity there for a while. Somehow, though, this eatery helped restore his equilibrium.

He slid onto a stool at the bar and picked up the menu.

After a few moments, another guy came in and took the next stool.

The man was wearing scruffy jeans, work boots and a heavy beige sweater that had several pulls in the knit. His brown hair was a little straggly around the edges. He looked to be in his early thirties, but his hands were rough and weathered. His whole appearance gave the impression that he did some kind of manual labor.

He gave Michael an assessing look. "You're not from around here."

"Right," Michael acknowledged.

"The crab cakes here are good. And they do a good job with the fries."

"Thanks for the tip."

A sad-faced man with thinning salt-and-pepper hair and a short, scraggly matching beard came walking along behind the bar toward them. He was wearing a plaid shirt and a rumpled apron. "What'll you have?"

Michael ordered a cup of coffee, and then the crab cakes, coleslaw and fries.

The man on the next stool got the same thing, with beer instead of coffee. Apparently he wanted company because after the bartender poured a mug of coffee, he said, "Name's Phil Cardon. You here for long?"

"Michael Bryant. I'm taking a few days to visit the area."

"Vacation?"

Michael took a sip of his coffee before he answered. "I'm thinking about setting a novel here."

The man nodded. "Well, there's plenty you could write about."

"That sounds intriguing. Like what?"

The guy downed the rest of his beer and signaled the bartender for another one. Cardon lowered his voice and said, "Like Rufus there. Rufus Shea. His son died thirteen years ago, and he's never gotten over it."

"How did he die?"

"He was murdered. Out in the bog."

"You have a lot of murders around here?" he asked.

The man laughed. "Not so many."

Before Michael could ask another question, the guy launched into a monologue.

"This is a town of real contrasts. You've got your rich people who buy up the prime property. And they're likely to stay here only a few months out of the year. Well, not the Drakes. They live here all year round."

"Who are the Drakes?"

"Brandon Drake and his uncle Clifford. They have a lot of business interests. Shipping. The Drake Yacht Club. Stuff like that. They got offices in town and big houses on the creek. I just did some wallboard repairs for Clifford. A plum job."

"Uh-huh." Michael filed that away.

Rufus Shea came back with the crab cake platters. "Enjoy your meal," he said.

"Thanks."

Michael took a bite. "You're right. This is good."

"Told you," the other diner said. He took another swallow of beer. "People like the Drakes have the cash to pay you. But then there are the watermen who are having a hard time making ends meet now with the fishing industry going down the tubes."

"It is?"

"The crabbing and oyster businesses aren't so good anymore, because the bay's not getting any cleaner."

"Uh-huh."

Phil Cardon dipped a French fry in ketchup, bit off the end and chewed before continuing. "Guys like the Drakes can afford to pay what your work is worth. Not like the bed-and-breakfast owners. They haggle with you 'cause they watch every penny."

"They're not doing well?"

"The tourist industry is the main business in Jenkins Cove, and there's a lot of competition. Where are you staying?"

"The House of the Seven Gables."

He made a whistling sound. "Those two ladies are a little…" Instead of finishing the sentence, he held his hand flat and wiggled it.

"Yeah." Michael laughed. "You think they're just kooks? Or do they have some scam going?"

"The aunt's got some psycho…psycho something up in the attic."

"Psychomanteum," Michael said. "How do you know about it?"

"Everybody does. She showed it to you?"

"Not yet. A lady from town came to contact her dead husband."

The handyman snorted.

"You don't believe in ghosts."

"Naw."

Michael considered asking if Cardon had ever felt cold spots in the air or felt as if someone invisible was watching him. He decided to keep that question to himself.

CHELSEA LISTENED FOR THE SOUND of the door. The couple from Baltimore had come in a half hour ago, but Michael Bryant was still out.

There was no reason she should be waiting for him. Especially in light of the scene in the kitchen earlier this evening. She should keep as far away from him as she could get. A little difficult, since he was staying in the same house with her.

She glanced at the clock. It was almost nine. His car was still in the parking lot across the street, which meant he'd walked into town. She wondered what was he doing till nine o'clock. Was he the kind of man who solved problems with drink?

Or had something happened to him? That was a ridiculous assumption, she told herself. Yet she couldn't turn off the nagging feeling of impending doom.

She snorted. Impending doom. That was a pretty strong phrase. Yet since the night of her trip to Tilghman Island, she had felt hypersensitive, tuned to fears and worries that hovered below the surface of her consciousness.

She couldn't turn the sensations off. They lingered with her, much like the feelings she felt in her dreams. Feelings that someone was whispering to her, only she couldn't quite decode the message.

Now, for some reason she couldn't identify, Michael Bryant was part of the equation.

That made no sense. She didn't even know him. Why should she care about him?

Unable to talk herself out of her worry, she kept listening for the sound of the key. After a while, she walked downstairs, intending to sit in the living room. Instead she walked to the front hall and stared out the sidelight, watching the street.

No, watching for Michael Bryant.

"WHAT DO YOU THINK about the niece? Chelsea," Michael asked his dinner companion.

"She's pretty."

"Yeah."

"I'd ask her out, only she keeps to herself."

"Oh?" That hadn't exactly been Michael's experience. She'd been more than willing in the kitchen a while ago. Not that he would share that experience with a casual dinner companion.

Instead he said, "The aunt says Chelsea saw a ghost."

"More than one, the way I hear it."

"Yeah," Michael answered again. "But you think it's a bunch of crap."

A strange expression crossed Phil's face. "I do," he said, but he didn't sound perfectly sure.

The guy looked around as if he wondered who had been listening to the conversation.

"I'm talking too much," Phil said.

"Of course not."

He climbed off the bar stool, reached in his pocket and got out some bills, which he left on the counter. Then he turned and walked to the door, weaving a little, and Michael wondered what Phil had really wanted to say.

Rufus Shea came back, presumably to clear the plate away. He stopped and rubbed a hand against his scraggly beard. "I guess Phil was giving you an earful about Jenkins Cove."

"Yeah."

"People around here tend to be opinionated."

"I'm finding that out."

He wondered how much of the conversation Shea had heard—like the part about his son dying.

"Phil was bragging about working for the Drakes," Shea said.

"Mmm-hmm."

"They're the big cheeses here in town. Of course, since Brandon's wife died, he's kept mostly to himself. He was hurt bad in the accident."

"She was killed in an accident?"

"Car accident."

Maybe Brandon Drake would show up at the House of the Seven Gables to try and contact his dead wife through the psychomanteum. Or maybe he already had.

In the short time he'd been here, it felt as if all roads in Jenkins Cove led back to death—murder or accidental.

Chapter Six

Michael walked back the way he'd come. The Christmas lights still gave the shops along Main Street and in the town square a festive air.

Maybe he was avoiding going back to the B & B, but he kept walking through the shopping area, past the turnoff that would take him directly back to the House of the Seven Gables.

Finally, when he was on his way out of town, he turned around and took Carpenter, heading toward the town dock.

Once he left the shopping area, he realized he had his ears tuned for any unusual sounds. Did he hear footsteps behind him? He stopped and listened intently. If anyone was there, they stopped, too.

Had someone followed him from the Duck Blind, or even from the House of the Seven Gables? That would make more sense than ghosts hiding in the bushes. Well, more sense if you were trying to fit this evening into the pattern of reality.

But who would have a reason to be checking up on him?

He didn't know.

Could it be someone with an interest in the B & B? Like that real-estate guy, Ned Perry, who had come into the kitchen?

But what would he want with one of the guests?

As Michael turned over the possibilities in his mind, he found that he was walking faster than usual. When he realized what he was doing, he deliberately slowed his pace. No way was he going to let a ghost or anyone else chase him.

A ghost. Good Lord, was he really starting to think in those terms? Was the atmosphere of Jenkins Cove turning his mind to mush?

He gritted his teeth. If he was being honest with himself, he'd have to admit that somehow Jenkins Cove was affecting him in ways that he couldn't figure out. It was as if he'd crossed some invisible barrier into a world where the laws of the universe were different—and unpredictable.

Even as the thought surfaced in his mind, he scoffed at it. He'd been in some of the world's real hellholes. He wasn't going to let this small town on the Eastern Shore of Maryland get to him. More important, he was not going to leave until he'd accomplished his mission.

CHELSEA PUT ON HER COAT and stepped out the back door. She wasn't sure what she was doing out here. She just had the feeling that she should be outside.

Then, from where she stood on the back porch, she saw a figure walking along Carpenter Street. A man. As she stared at him, she was sure it was Michael Bryant.

Finally.

A little speech played through her mind. She wanted to tell him that she was worried about him. That he should have told her if he was going to come in so late. And he should be coming straight back to the House of the Seven Gables. He shouldn't be making a detour to the dock area.

Then she told herself those thoughts were so out of bounds that they shouldn't even have surfaced in her head.

She wasn't his wife.

Lord, where had that come from?

He didn't owe her any explanations. Just because she'd fallen into his arms and kissed him didn't mean that they had a relationship.

She was about to go back inside when she saw a little gust of wind hit him as he walked across the bridge toward the dock.

He lurched unsteadily. Then she saw headlights barreling up the street in back of him, the car moving much too fast as it approached the bridge.

It looked as though Michael didn't know the car was there, maybe because the wind had picked up.

But the vehicle was heading right for him.

She found herself running and shouting at the same time, "Michael. Watch out! Michael."

He glanced up and must have caught the twin beams streaming past him.

Luckily his reflexes were good. The speeding car was only inches from him when he jumped out of the way. But he was already so close to the edge of the little creek that when he jumped, there was nowhere to go but into the brackish water.

"Michael!" she shouted again, hurtling down the path toward the creek that separated the B & B from the dock. From the corner of her eye she saw the car careen along the lane, then turn and head back toward Main Street. But she wasn't focused on that.

The man in the water was her main concern. The creek probably wasn't deep. But it was lined with rocks to keep the banks from eroding, and if he'd hit his head when he went over the side, he could be in trouble.

"Michael, are you all right?" She couldn't see him, and she wished she had a flashlight.

When he didn't answer, her heart leaped into her throat. Then she heard a splash followed by a scrambling noise. As she climbed down the rocks, she saw a figure climbing up.

She waved, then reached out her hand. "Michael. Over here, Michael. Thank God."

Grasping a large rock with one hand, she leaned over and reached down with the other.

His fingers fumbled for hers. Then they locked on, and he hauled himself up.

In soaking-wet clothes, he weighed a ton, but in the light from the dock area, she saw that he'd managed to keep his head out of the water.

When he reached the edge of the pavement, he wavered on unsteady legs.

Chelsea grabbed his arm. "Are you all right?"

"Yeah," Michael answered. "If you don't count wet and cold." He looked in the direction where the car had vanished. "Is that a street?"

"Not one that's used very often."

"I don't suppose you got the license number?"

"Sorry. I was looking at you—not the car."

Michael's teeth started to chatter.

"You have to get inside," Chelsea said.

He looked at her, registering the fact that she'd been outside. "What were you doing out here?"

"I go for walks."

The explanation sounded lame, but he wasn't going to call her on it—not when she'd probably saved his life with her warning. "Lucky for me that you saw the car."

"Come on inside." She tugged on his arm, leading him toward the house, and he didn't resist. He needed to get out of the elements.

"Do people around here usually drive like that?" he asked.

"Not usually. Maybe it was a tourist."

"From my point of view, it looked like someone was deliberately trying to run me over."

She winced, craning her neck back toward the turnoff where the car had disappeared.

"Why would someone try to run you down? Do you have enemies?" she asked.

"Not that I know of. And certainly not in Jenkins Cove. I just got here." He tipped his head to the side. "Is this a dangerous town?"

"I didn't think so. Until the murder," she clipped out as she marched steadily toward the house.

She stepped onto the screened porch, and he followed her into the kitchen, dripping on the tile floor.

She eyed him critically. "You need to take off your clothes."

He managed to laugh. "Is that an invitation?"

"Very funny." She gave him an annoyed look. "I have some of those white bathrobes we give guests."

She walked into a laundry room off the kitchen, then emerged with a robe. "Get undressed in there. And leave the clothes. I'll wash them."

"The jacket's got to go to the cleaner's, I think."

He stepped into the laundry room, closed the door behind him and took everything off—except his wet briefs because he didn't want to leave her his underwear. Then he put on the robe and got his damp wallet, keys and change out of his pockets.

He was feeling awkward when he came back to the kitchen, but she was very matter-of-fact as she handed him a steaming mug. "Hot chocolate."

"Thanks." He took a sip. "This is good."

"And it will warm you up." As she said that, she looked away, and he knew she was sharing the awkward feeling.

"I hate to put you to any trouble," he mumbled.

"I have to do a load of wash anyway."

"I left my shoes over by the door."

"That's fine."

"You should get into bed. Get warm."

"Yeah," he answered, thinking that every word that came out of her mouth seemed to have a double meaning, although she probably didn't intend it that way. "Thanks for being there. I'll see you at breakfast."

"Maybe not."

"Oh?"

"We have a woman from town who helps us. I'm probably going to be in my studio." She walked toward the front of the house; he followed, the mug warming his hands.

She hurried toward the stairs, leaving before he could think of anything else to say to keep her there.

They still hadn't resolved the kiss in the kitchen. Now it looked as if they weren't going to get a chance to talk in the morning, either.

He set down the mug on a hall table and let himself into his room. He'd been going to check his e-mail. Instead he took everything out of his wallet and set the damp leather on the shelf above the radiator. Then he washed off the creek water in the shower before climbing under the covers.

Taking a sip of the hot chocolate, he replayed the incident with the car. Had someone really tried to kill him? Or had it been an accident? Maybe a drunken tourist driving along the dock.

He went over it again and again in his mind. But the only conclusion he could come to was that he'd been damn lucky Chelsea had been outside.

He was tired, but he had trouble getting to sleep. He tossed and turned most of the night, then finally fell asleep just before dawn.

He slept until nine, barely giving him time to make the breakfast hours at the B & B.

True to her word, Chelsea wasn't there. But her helper, who introduced herself as Barbara, had apparently been waiting for him. She handed him his shirt and pants, freshly washed.

"Thank you. Thank Chelsea for me."

"Certainly. We put your shoes on the radiator. They're dry, too."

"Yeah. I did the same with my wallet." He took the clothing back to his room. When he returned, he poured himself a cup of coffee from the sideboard, then ate a piece of quiche along with a blueberry muffin.

Neither of the Caldwells showed up while he was there, so he put on a heavy sweater and walked to the dry cleaner's, where he left his jacket. They had an expensive four-hour service, so he'd be able to get the jacket before the evening chill.

Next he went back to the dock. With a small digital camera, he snapped some pictures where he'd gone into the water. Then he took more pictures along Center Street and Main Street, which was bustling with tourists.

In some of the shops, he pretended he was interested in local souvenirs like duck decoys, little lighthouses and books on the waterman's way of life. He also managed to start conversations about the woman who had seen the ghost.

He didn't find anyone who hadn't read the story in the paper or heard about it.

"So, what do you think?" he asked a gray-haired woman who ran a candy shop.

She gave him a narrow-eyed look. "I think it's bad for business. There are fewer tourists here than in the past couple of years."

"But she had to report the murder," he argued, finding himself suddenly defending Chelsea.

The woman shuddered. "Yes, but she should have kept ghosts out of it. Murder is bad enough. Ghosts just make it worse."

Michael left with a bag of hard candies, wondering about his motives. Was he being objective or merely looking to bolster his case against Chelsea?

As he stepped onto the street again, the back of his neck tingled. Apparently that was going to be a regular occurrence as long as he was in town. Casually, he stopped to look in the window of a real-estate company. Using the reflection of the glass, he tried to see if someone was following him. But the street was crowded, and he couldn't pick out anyone in particular, even when he walked all the way down the block, pausing frequently to surreptitiously look behind him.

After crossing the street, he wandered into the Chesapeake Gallery, where he stopped short when he saw a painting he recognized. He'd seen it on Chelsea's Web site. It was a landscape scene that he assumed was near Jenkins Cove. He saw a marsh with cattails and a mist rising from the ground. In the background was a grand house with balconies and multiple chimneys.

A small woman with dyed black hair noticed his interest. "That's by Chelsea Caldwell, one of our local artists."

"It's very evocative," he allowed. "Is that a real house?"

"The Drake mansion."

"Um."

The Drakes again. He'd heard about them last

night from that guy in the Duck Blind—Phil Cardon. Maybe they were like the local nobility.

He wondered if the house was really in back of a marsh, or if she'd moved elements around to create the effect she wanted.

When the woman asked if he was interested in buying the painting, he disappointed her by saying that he wasn't going to purchase anything until the end of his stay in town.

He walked around the gallery and saw several more paintings by Chelsea. New works, he assumed, since they hadn't been on the Web site. She was good. He could see why she'd done well in Baltimore. He hoped she sold as well in Jenkins Cove.

That thought brought him up short. He kept letting his feelings interfere with business.

It happened again when he returned to the B & B, hoping to see Chelsea. When she wasn't anywhere around, he fought a stab of disappointment.

He could have made himself comfortable in the living room. Instead he got in his car and drove to the approximate location of the murder. Pulling onto the shoulder, he climbed out and snapped some more pictures.

Keeping busy, he returned to town and found the owner of a fishing boat who was willing to take him for a ride and point out local landmarks. Some creek, he thought. It was almost a hundred yards wide.

He snapped pictures of the Drake estates, both of

which were on the bay, separated by a spit of land. One of them was definitely the house he'd seen in the painting.

From the fisherman, he found out that it was Brandon's house in the painting. So, was Chelsea friends with the local nobility?

Chelsea. He kept coming back to her. Even when he wasn't asking questions about the lady who'd seen the ghost.

Thinking that he was acting like a teenager with a crush, he deliberately walked in the other direction. After picking up his jacket at the dry cleaner's, he had an early dinner that kept him away from the B & B during the wine and cheese hour.

It was dark by the time he came back, and nobody was on the first floor. He returned to his room, got out his laptop and uploaded the pictures he'd taken, then settled back to look at a slide show.

The first two images seemed normal, but he got a jolt when he clicked on the third one, a view along Center Street. While the previous scenes had looked bright and sunny, in this one, mist seemed to hang over the area. The same mist that he hadn't seen when he'd been out for his walk.

A chill skittered along his nerve endings. It was as if he'd captured something strange in the atmosphere of Jenkins Cove.

He paged rapidly through the rest of the innocuous pictures he'd taken until he got to the one taken in the swampy area where Chelsea had seen the murder. There again he found the same kind of foggy patches that he'd encountered on the Center Street image.

What was he seeing? Some trick of the light? An atmospheric disturbance that was only apparent on a digital image?

Or was there something wrong with his camera? Would he get the same kinds of distortions with a camera that used film?

He spent a long time studying the images, feeling stranger and stranger as he did so.

Finally he turned off the computer and spent another restless night. His dreams were filled with foggy images and Chelsea.

Chapter Seven

When Michael got up the next morning, he felt fairly certain that Chelsea was avoiding him. He had to change that. Because he wanted to get her to tell him ghost stories...or because he just wanted to see her?

In the dining room Sophie greeted him warmly. "How are you enjoying your stay in Jenkins Cove?"

"Fine." He poured himself a cup of coffee from the sideboard, then brought it to the table that had been set for him with silver, china and a basket of freshly baked muffins.

"Where's Chelsea?" he asked as he unfolded his napkin.

Aunt Sophie answered in a chipper voice. "She's been anxious to get a painting finished. She's up in her studio."

She bustled out of the room and returned with a slice of cheese frittata, bacon and cubes of cantaloupe.

As soon as he'd finished eating, Sophie came back

into the dining room, and he wondered if she had been waiting for him to leave so she could clean up.

Instead she said, "I can take you up to see her studio, if you'd like."

He thought about that for a moment. Chelsea probably wouldn't appreciate his barging in. If her aunt were with him, however, she couldn't complain.

"I'd like that," he answered.

Sophie led him to the third floor of the B & B. Several closed doors lined the hallway.

A sudden thought struck him, and he asked, "Is the psychomanteum up here?"

"Why, yes. Would you like to see it?" She sounded delighted that he'd mentioned her pet project, and he was suddenly on the alert, wondering if she was going to try and sell him shares or something.

"Okay," he answered guardedly.

She gave him an encouraging smile. "I won't leave you in there."

"You think I'm afraid to stay by myself?" he snapped, then was sorry he'd let his tension get the better of him.

"Some people are."

"Well, I'm not," he said firmly, sounding to his own ears like a little kid proclaiming he wasn't afraid to enter a haunted house.

"Jenkins Cove is noted for psychic phenomena," she said.

"Why?"

"Because we have such a long history. This was one of the first places settled in Maryland, due to our many rivers and creeks. In colonial times, water was the easiest way to get around."

"The town didn't grow much," he said.

"That's because we're isolated from the mainland by the Chesapeake Bay. The water that was an advantage in the early days turned out to be just the opposite as people moved farther west."

Sophie opened a door and switched on a light, then stepped into a room that was bathed in black. It emitted an eerie feel. The ceiling was painted black, the walls were hung with black curtains and a dark carpet covered the floor. In the middle of the room sat a chair facing an enormous rectangular mirror framed in ornate gold. It leaned against one of the side walls. Various antique chests and small tables decorated the room, all of them decked out with pillar candles and slender tapers in elaborate candelabra.

Aunt Sophie saw him eyeing them. "You have no idea how hard it is to get unscented candles," she said. "I don't want this place smelling like vanilla or cinnamon or something like that. So I started making them myself. Then I did get into the scented ones for downstairs."

"Right," he murmured. His gaze flicked to the heavy mirror and the curtains. "Who set this up?"

"I did. Well, it's all my idea, but I hired Phil

Cardon to paint the ceiling, hang the curtain rods and carry the mirror up here. I sewed the curtains myself," she added proudly.

Suddenly, the fixture in the ceiling dimmed. With the black curtains and paint, the room became much darker—and spookier. He jerked around to see Sophie working a dimmer switch.

"People who use the room adjust the light the way it's most comfortable for them," she said.

"Uh-huh. Do people really communicate with ghosts in here?"

"Yes."

"How do they know?"

"The spirits speak to them."

"How do they know it's not their imaginations working overtime?"

"They have faith." She dragged in a breath and let it out. "I've spoken to my sister in here. She died fifty years ago."

"How do you know it was her?"

"She told me things that only the two of us would remember."

He could have argued that the conversation was coming from Sophie's imagination, but he didn't want to challenge her. If it made her happy to think she had spoken to her sister, that was okay by him. Just so she didn't have a microphone in here where she pretended to be speaking for the dead. Yeah, he'd better check on that.

"If you want to have a session, just let me know."

"I don't know any of the ghosts around here."

"Well, the spirit world has no physical boundaries."

It would be a cold day in hell before he took her up on the offer to contact the dead.

When they stepped back into the hall, he immediately felt some of the tightness go out of his throat. "Chelsea's studio is down the hall," she said.

Instantly the tightness was back, but for a different reason. He was going to see Chelsea again for the first time since he'd stood in the kitchen in a borrowed bathrobe.

Sophie led the way to the opposite end of the house where the hall turned a corner.

As they stepped to their right, light flooded in through a huge window with a half transom addition above the rectangular section.

It took a moment for his eyes to adjust to the brightness. When they did, he could see Chelsea in a room right in front of them. She was standing at an easel, dabbing paint on a canvas. An artist's pallet sat on a tall narrow table beside her.

When she looked up and registered their presence, her eyes widened in shock. Was she thinking she could avoid him? Or was it unusual for her aunt to bring a guest into her private space?

"What…what are you doing here?" she asked, her gaze accusing him of stepping over an invisible boundary.

He kept his tone neutral. "Your aunt offered to show me your studio, and I took her up on it."

She regarded him for several heartbeats, then gave Sophie an annoyed look. "I'm supposed to be working. You know I like my private time."

"Of course. But Mr. Bryant seemed so interested," Sophie said with enthusiasm.

"Can I see what you're painting?" he asked.

Her mouth tightened.

"I'd like to see it, too," Sophie said.

When Chelsea gave a little shrug and stepped back, Michael and Sophie took up positions in front of the painting.

The canvas showed downtown Jenkins Cove on a winter evening, with all the shops decked out for the holidays. It was very much like the way the street had looked when he'd walked down to the Duck Blind, only in the painting, snow was lightly falling, dusting the road and shops.

"It's very good. Charming," he said, meaning it. "I love the way you've done the lights. They seem to glow."

She looked at him as if to determine whether he was sincere.

"Chelsea is donating it to a charity auction," Sophie said. "That's why she's in a hurry—so it can dry in time for the big Christmas party."

"I'm about finished," Chelsea said.

"Mmm-hum." What was it about these women

that reduced him to such replies? Casting around for something else to say, he asked, "Where do you get your ideas for paintings?"

She gave him a strange look. "People ask me that all the time. But I wouldn't expect the question from you."

"Why not?"

"Because you're a writer. Where do you get *your* ideas?"

He flushed. "Right. But ideas for books are different."

"Why?"

He fumbled for an answer. "You're working in a visual medium. I'm not. Each painting you do is like a snapshot. You don't get to show any progression."

"Sometimes I do, like when I paint the same scene at different times of the day or different seasons."

"True."

Sophie leaped into the conversation. "I showed Mr. Bryant the psychomanteum."

Chelsea's head snapped toward her aunt. "And he thought it was a waste of time," she guessed.

"I think he sees it as artificial," the aunt answered before Michael could give his own opinion. Changing the subject completely, she said, "I think you should take advantage of the nice weather. Take him to the old warehouse down by Smugglers Bend where he can experience something real."

Chelsea blinked. "Why?"

"Because it's supposed to be haunted. It's something real, not a room that an old lady set up. He can see if he picks up any vibrations."

"Is that a challenge?" Michael asked.

"Yes," Sophie answered.

"Why don't *you* take him?" Chelsea suggested.

"I have some baking to do. And, of course, I'm not as spry as I used to be. It's a trip best undertaken by young people."

"I can go on my own," Michael said, glancing at Chelsea and then away.

"You'll never find it," she was quick to answer, and then her face contorted as she probably realized that she'd basically offered to take him.

"Let's go," Michael said, before she figured out an excuse to change her mind.

She looked as though she wanted to protest, but apparently she wasn't going to be rude to a guest in front of her aunt. With a little sigh, she took off the smock she was wearing over her shirt and jeans, then went to the sink in the corner and washed her hands.

As they all started downstairs, she asked, "You really want to go to the warehouse?"

"Aunt Sophie thinks it will be good for me."

"You catch on real quick, young man," the woman in question answered.

When they descended to the first floor, Michael went to get his jacket and his camera. Chelsea was waiting for him when he came back to the front hall.

She eyed the jacket, which looked a lot better than it had after his dunk in the creek. "You stopped at the dry cleaner's?" she asked.

"Uh-huh. The coat's as good as new."

She gave him a long look, the first halfway friendly gesture of the morning. "And you're okay?" she asked softly.

"Yes."

"Good."

They climbed into her small car. "I never did actually thank you for saving my life."

"No problem."

"Maybe not for you. But it made a great deal of difference to me."

He saw that she couldn't quite suppress a grin.

AS THE WATCHER SAW THE PAIR exit the House of the Seven Gables, he pressed back into the shadows of the storage shed.

Michael Bryant and Chelsea Caldwell together.

Very interesting.

What were they up to now?

He'd thought he could simplify his job by running down Bryant on his way back from the Duck Blind the other night. But Chelsea had saved him.

Since Bryant had come to town, the guy had been asking a lot of questions. Mainly about ghosts. But that might not be his main interest.

Was he really an investigative reporter…or was he an undercover cop or a private eye?

The sooner Bryant left Jenkins Cove, the better— either under his own power, or on a stretcher headed for the medical examiner. Either way was absolutely fine.

But right now the two of them were up to something.

When Chelsea pulled out of her parking spot, the watcher walked back to his own vehicle, which was over at the other side of the town parking lot. He didn't need to keep them in sight. He'd already put a transponder on Chelsea's car. And on Bryant's, too.

So all he had to do was turn on his GPS, and he could follow at a discreet distance.

MICHAEL MIGHT have gotten Chelsea to grin, but now that they were in her car, he could have cut the silence with a knife. As they turned onto Main Street, he heard himself say, "You've been avoiding me."

"Don't you think that's the best policy?" she snapped.

"I don't know."

"I don't usually end up in clinches with men I barely know," she said.

Keeping his voice light, he answered, "I thought that getting me to move out of the path of a speeding car showed you cared."

"That was just common courtesy."

"Okay." After another few minutes of silence he said, "I'm only going to be here for a few more days."

"Are you suggesting that we have a fling while you're in town?" she asked, her voice tight.

"Come on. That's not what I said at all. I just think we should try to get along with each other."

She nodded.

"So, have you lived in Jenkins Cove all your life?" he asked.

She glanced at him, then turned back to the road. "I grew up in Baltimore."

"How did you start painting?"

"I always liked to do it. My parents left me some money—enough to live on for a few years while I established my career."

"Your parents are dead? I'm sorry."

"Losing them was hard. But it made me self-sufficient."

"Yeah. My dad died when I was little. My mom wasn't so great at coping."

"I'm sorry." She paused, then commented, "So I take it you didn't have a happy childhood."

"No. We didn't have a lot of money. And my mom didn't spend it wisely." He heard the tightness in his voice. "What about your childhood?"

She shrugged. "It was pretty typical."

Except for seeing a ghost, he thought.

"So why did you agree to take me to the old warehouse?" he asked.

"The place has always had a bad reputation. I want to find out why. And I don't want to go alone."

"You're trying to prove something to yourself?"

"Maybe. Are you?"

"Maybe," he admitted.

"Were you trying to prove something by going into the psychomanteum?"

"I was curious."

"Uh-huh."

"People really think they've communicated with loved ones?" he asked.

"Yes."

"Do you think it's true?"

"I don't know."

He didn't press his luck by asking about her personal experiences with ghosts. He'd come to Jenkins Cove prepared to interrogate her. Since arriving, he'd been having a lot of second thoughts.

She wasn't what he'd expected at all, and he was struggling to adjust his thinking.

They drove along the highway toward Tilghman Island. A few miles outside town, Chelsea slowed, then turned right onto a one-lane gravel road.

It was an isolated location. Trees grew close on either side, and he saw there were places where the ends of branches had been hit. "The warehouse is not used?"

"That's right."

"But someone has been down here."

"How do you know?"

"A vehicle lopped off the ends of some branches."

"Maybe it was teenagers looking for a deserted place to have—" She stopped before she said the word *sex*. "You know what I mean."

She clamped her hands on the wheel, and he had the feeling she wished she hadn't brought up the topic.

"I thought that this place had a bad reputation," he said.

"Kids would ignore it."

He wasn't so sure, but he wasn't going to argue with her. The road took a bend, and when they emerged from the foliage, he saw the blue gleam of water in the sunlight and a building ahead of them. It was constructed of weathered wood, with some of the boards missing on the sides. From what he could see, it was partly on land and partly sticking into the cattails that lined the shore.

She drove up to a weed-strewn parking area and cut the engine.

They were facing a wide doorway, covered by a sliding door.

Michael eyed the building. "This place is pretty run-down. What was it used for?"

"Fifty years ago, it was a shipping depot and a warehouse. But there's not much direct shipping to Jenkins Cove anymore."

They climbed out, and he slipped his hands into

his pockets as they stood facing the building, bracing against the wind that had sprung up.

This was just a run-down warehouse, he told himself, yet he couldn't shake the feeling that there was something more here. When he glanced at Chelsea, he saw that she had her arms wrapped around her shoulders. So either she, too, was reacting to the place, or she was reacting to being alone with him.

"I want to see what's inside," he said.

She gave him a startled look, and he saw her swallow. "Okay."

The sun had gone behind a cloud, and wind buffeted them as they walked toward the double doors.

"Is it safe to go in there?" he asked.

"I guess we'll find out." She marched up to the door and gave it a tug. Nothing happened.

"It's probably rusty." He stepped to the barrier and pulled on the handle. The door gave a little, and when he kept up the pressure, it rolled to the side.

The interior was mostly in shadow, although there were patches of weak sunlight shining through.

For long seconds, neither of them moved, and he felt his nerves jumping.

"There's something in there," Chelsea whispered.

"What?"

"I don't know."

"Let's find out."

"No." She grabbed his arm, but he pulled away and took a step forward, then another.

He didn't turn, but he heard Chelsea following him.

The floor of the old building was made of cracked cement, with a few hardy weeds growing up through the cracks.

Something on the floor glinted in the sunlight, and he walked forward to see what it was.

As he reached the center of the room, a white and gray cloud of whirring, flapping ghosts came rushing toward them.

Chelsea gasped. Michael caught her in his arms, covering her head with one of his hands as a flock of seabirds flapped around the interior, then found their way out through the holes in the roof.

The large room was suddenly silent again. But everything had changed in the space of a heartbeat. Once again, he was holding Chelsea in his arms. And once again, he marveled at how good that felt.

He murmured her name, and she raised her head. Their eyes met, and he silently asked her the question.

"Don't," she whispered. "Don't kiss me."

He ached to cover her mouth with his, but he wouldn't go against her wishes. Still, he kept his arms around her. "Why not?" Male arrogance had him adding, "We both want to."

"Yes," she acknowledged. "But not here. They're watching."

He looked around. "There's nobody here."

"Can't you sense it?" she asked in a hushed voice.

He stood very still, feeling the beating of his own

heart and imagining he could feel hers, too. Above that rhythm of life, he detected something else.

The air in this place was thick. Not with dust or any kind of man-made particles. It was thick with a kind of energy that seemed to swirl around him and press in against him, making it hard to breathe.

Like the night he'd walked along Center Street, he felt a coldness in the air.

He could explain that part, though. In here, the roof of the building was keeping out the sun, so naturally it was colder.

"The air," Chelsea whispered. "It's cold and thick. And there are voices."

"Voices?"

"Don't you hear them?"

He went very still, listening. He thought he heard the whispering of the wind, but that was all.

"What are they saying?" he asked.

"I don't know. Not for sure. But it's important."

The sounds around him had taken on an urgency. Then, once again, he tried to put down the uneasy feelings to his overactive imagination.

He dragged in a breath and caught a faint odor wafting toward him. The odor of unwashed bodies. Or was his imagination working overtime again?

Chelsea had turned into him, burying her face against his chest.

He stroked his hands over her back and shoulders, comforting her and drawing comfort in return.

When he felt her shiver, he clasped her more tightly.

"It's okay," he said, not actually sure what he meant. All right to hear the whispering voices? Or all right to dismiss them?

"I can't stay in here any longer."

He nodded, unwilling to voice his agreement. "Give me a second."

"What?"

He stepped away from her, then strode to the place where he'd seen something on the floor. Stooping, he picked up a shiny piece of metal. A woman's earring.

"Someone was here," he said.

"Kids," she said again, but she didn't sound perfectly sure.

He'd brought his camera. Pulling it out of his pocket, he snapped several pictures, wondering if they'd come out like the strange ones from his trip around town.

He didn't tell Chelsea about those, as he slung his arm around her again and led her back toward the door.

They stepped into the open air, and he took a deep breath. A dark cloud had slid across the sun, so that the adjustment from the gloom wasn't as sharp as it would have been.

That was probably why Michael saw a flash of movement in the bushes. And then a figure was running away from the warehouse.

"Stay here," he shouted, calling the order over his shoulder as he took off after the fleeing figure.

"Come back!"

"I'll be okay." As he ran, he tried to see where the watcher had gone.

It had looked like a man, but he couldn't be sure. Michael headed for the spot where the guy had disappeared into a screen of vegetation. No one was there, but the weeds at the side of a pine tree were crushed down, as though someone had been standing there.

He thought he detected a path someone had made through the underbrush. He followed it, trying to catch up with whoever had been watching them.

Then he stepped on a patch of ground that gave way under his feet—and he was falling into blackness.

Chapter Eight

Chelsea heard Michael call out. It sounded as though he was in trouble.

With her heart blocking her windpipe, she went dashing into the woods, heading for the place where he'd disappeared into the underbrush.

She heard him shouting at her, but she couldn't see him.

"Chelsea. Stay back."

She stopped in her tracks, her heart pounding. "Michael, where are you?"

"I fell into a trap. Watch out."

She sucked in a sharp breath. "Where?"

"Over here. Be careful. There could be more of them."

"I can't see you. Keep talking to me. Are you all right?"

He hesitated for a moment. "Yes."

"You're not sure."

"Nothing major."

Her stomach knotted. Was he lying to her? She wasn't going to find out until she got to him.

"Keep talking."

"I'm below ground level. So be careful not to fall into a trap—" His breath caught.

"What?"

"That guy. He could still be here."

She stopped short, wanting to protest. But he was right. "What should I do?" she called in a harsh whisper.

"Get out of here."

"No."

She scanned the woods. Someone could leap out of the bushes at any time, yet she couldn't leave Michael. It sounded as though he was hurt. And if the guy came back, he'd be a sitting duck.

She waited for several moments. It seemed as though they were alone. Of course, the man could simply be waiting to grab her. But if so, why hadn't he already done it?

She'd figured out Michael's approximate location. Following a narrow trail, she kept walking until she came to a place where she saw a mat of leaves on the ground and a ragged hole at one side.

Creeping closer, she went down on her hands and knees and peered into the pit. Michael was at the bottom, looking up at her.

"Are you all right?" she asked.

"I whacked my knee on the way down. No big deal."

"Can you climb out?"

"Not on my own. The wall crumbles when I grab it."

"What do you want me to do?"

"I don't suppose you carry rope in your car."

"No."

He sighed. "See if you can find a fallen branch. Something I can use to pull myself up."

She stepped away, surveying the area, and saw that the covering of the pit was partially made of pine boughs. "Maybe we can use these," she said. As she spoke she reached out to grasp one of the branches and almost lost her balance.

"Watch out," Michael shouted.

"I am." This time she was more cautious, tugging on the end of a branch and pulling it toward her. It slid forward, and she maneuvered it over the hole where he could see it.

"Will that work?" she asked.

"I hope so. Can you turn it the other way, so the branches are facing upward?"

"Yes." She eased it down into the pit, then tugged at another branch, which she lowered to Michael.

He arranged the two branches, propping them against the wall of earth. Then he looked up at her. "Better stand back. I'm going to do this fast."

She took a step back, watching as he tested the

horizontal branches sticking out from the main bough. Then he began to scramble upward, using the two sets of limbs as a ladder.

He had almost made it to the top when she heard a crack and saw him drop back down. Leaping forward, she reached over the edge and grabbed his jacket, pulling upward.

She wouldn't have been able to hold him up by herself. But he must have still had one foot on a branch, and her grip was enough to keep him from falling back into the pit. He plowed ahead, practically leaping the last few feet so that they tumbled together onto the ground.

Michael landed atop her, panting and wincing.

"Are you okay?"

"The damn knee. Did I hurt you?"

"No."

He rolled to his side and looked into her eyes. "That's the second time you saved me. I mean, if you hadn't been here, I would have been stuck in that trap until whoever dug it and covered the pine boughs with brush came back to see what he caught."

She winced, alarm written on her features as she stared at him. Lifting her hand, she touched his cheek.

That touch, and the look in her eyes, undid him.

Without giving her time to protest, he leaned forward, finding her mouth with his. The kiss was a celebration. Celebration that he'd made it out of the pit, and that she was here in his arms.

He turned his head first one way and then the other, devouring her with an urgency that no longer surprised him.

No matter why he had come to Jenkins Cove, no matter what he had started out thinking about her, everything had changed.

He had assumed she was running some kind of scam. Or at the very least, trying to make herself seem important. But nothing could be further from the truth. She was so totally open and honest that the knowledge made his guts ache.

She could have walked away from him a few minutes ago. Instead she'd almost tumbled into the trap as she tried to help him get out.

That was the kind of person she was. If she thought she'd seen a ghost, then that was what she truly thought. He still didn't know if he believed in phantoms, but he understood that strange things had been happening to him since he'd arrived in Jenkins Cove. Things that he couldn't explain in any of the rational terms that he'd used all his life.

Falling for her was no exception. He'd never let a woman sweep him off his feet. But it had happened with Chelsea Caldwell. And it had happened totally against his will.

He kissed her with an urgency that might have surprised him, except that he had given up fighting what he was feeling. He hadn't known her long, and maybe the realization that he had been unfair to her fueled his need. He wanted to apologize. But there was nothing he could say without getting himself into deep trouble. He could only show her what he was feeling.

So he devoured her mouth, using his lips and teeth and tongue. He slipped his hands under her coat, moving them restlessly over her as he drank in her sweetness.

He felt her breathing accelerate. Felt her move her body restlessly against his, wordlessly telling him that they were in perfect harmony.

Flames leaped inside him. Flames that threatened to consume him. He wanted her with an urgency that took his breath away. With an unsteady hand, he pushed her coat out of the way, so that he could cup her breast through her shirt and slide his hand back and forth across the hardened tip while he nibbled at her jaw, then the slender column of her neck and her collarbone.

She tasted wonderful. Felt wonderful. He knew he had been aching to do this since he'd kissed her in the kitchen.

"Michael," she murmured, her hands just as restless as she ran her fingers through his hair, then under his coat and shirt so that she could stroke his ribs, his back. Her intimate touch almost sent him over the edge.

Though they were racing rapidly toward the point of no return, he allowed himself to revel in the heat of their passion for a only few moments longer. Then he lifted his mouth and forced himself to put a few inches of air between them.

Her eyes had been closed. They blinked open, and she stared at him, looking dazed and confused. That look tore at him.

"Michael?"

"I'm taking advantage of you," he said, hearing the raw sound of his own voice.

"No."

"We've only known each other for a few days. This is going too fast—for you." Her wounded look made him gather her close. "I want you," he whispered. "More than I've ever wanted any other woman. But I'm not going to make love to you out here in the woods. Certainly not when someone could be out there watching or coming back."

Her sudden look of alarm made his insides twist.

"You're right. What was I thinking?" She sat up and glanced around as though she expected someone to leap out of the bushes.

He sat up, as well, then stood, testing his knee and wincing.

"Michael!"

"I just need some ice to keep it from swelling up."

"Which we won't get here. We'd better go home."

"Yeah. But first…" He pulled her into his arms again, sliding his hands down her body, cupping her bottom so that he could press her against his erection. He needed to feel her there. And he needed her to feel what she had done to him.

"I'm going to make love to you," he said in a gritty voice. "That's a promise. But not until you know me better. I'm not going to sweep you along on a tide of passion. I want you to make a conscious decision about what we're doing."

She tipped her head back, staring up at him. "Did I have the misfortune to get tangled up with a gentleman?"

"I hope so," he muttered, feeling the weight of the confession he should make to her. But not yet. Not until he had time to think about what he was going to say.

She reached to stroke back the lock of hair that had fallen across his forehead. "I think I can cope with that."

"Good." He knitted his fingers with hers and started back the way they'd come, trying not to limp.

And as he walked, he scanned the ground and woods around them, watching for sudden movement and for more traps. There were none on the way back to the parking area.

As they stood beside the car, she gave him a critical inspection. "Your jacket's dirty."

"Back to the cleaner's."

The comment made her frown. "What's happening? I mean—first the murder, then someone tried to run you over and now this."

He felt his face harden. "I don't know. I saw someone watching us, and I'm going to find out who it is."

"Not a ghost," she whispered.

He looked back over his shoulder. "A ghost didn't dig a hole in the ground and cover it with brush. A ghost didn't lead me right to it, so I'd fall in."

"Should we call Chief Hammer?"

"Let's stop by the police station."

"You want to see him in person?" she asked.

He caught the tone of her voice. "You don't think that's a good idea?"

"I don't feel comfortable around him."

"Why not?"

She raised her head and gave him a direct look, then stared off into the distance as she began to speak again. "Something happened when I was a kid." She huffed in a breath and let it out. "You just mentioned ghosts. When I was ten, I thought I saw the ghost of a woman when I was at a friend's house."

He felt a shiver go over his skin. He knew all about that. But now she was telling him. Should he admit that he'd investigated her? "Did you?" he managed to say.

"I don't know," she said in a low voice. "I saw a woman. I'm sure of that much. Maybe she ran away," she said uncertainly. Her voice hardened when she added, "But my friend told people and before I knew it, everybody in town was talking about it. Hammer was on the police force then. He wasn't the chief, but he was an officer.

"Before that summer, I used to come to Jenkins Cove all the time. After that, I begged to stay home. I would have stayed away permanently, except that Aunt Sophie needed me to help her run the House of the Seven Gables." She dragged in a breath and let it out. "So don't be surprised if Hammer blows us off."

"If he comes out here, he'll see the pit. To my way of thinking, it looks like it's a security measure."

"And he'll probably tell you it's for hunting deer."

Michael laughed, then sobered again. "We should tell the chief. And I don't want to do it at the house, because I don't want to worry your aunt."

"You're right. If we make a report at the station, she doesn't have to know about your falling into the trap." She gave his coat another critical look, then began brushing it off with her hand, getting off the worst of the dirt.

He reached to fish a piece of grass out of her hair, then picked more off her coat. "I guess we look presentable enough."

They climbed into the car, and she sat for a moment without turning the key. "This is totally outside my experience," she finally said. "I mean us."

"Yeah."

"What would you call it?"

He laughed. "Strong attraction." Then he sobered. "But it's more on my part. I was attracted to you right away. The more I get to know you, the more I like you."

She flushed, then said in a low voice, "You don't know me very well."

"I mean to change that. What's your favorite food?" he asked in a teasing voice.

"Chocolate-chip brownies."

"Good choice. And what's your favorite color?"

"Blue. What's yours?"

"Blue."

"Honestly?"

"Yeah. See, we have something important in common."

"What's the best thing you remember from your childhood?"

He didn't even have to think about that. "Discovering Robert Heinlein. I loved reading his books. What about you?"

"The acrylic paint set my parents gave me when I was twelve."

"What about brothers and sisters?" he asked. That was something he hadn't checked on.

"I was an only child."

"Me, too. Was that good or bad for you?"

"Good. I got a lot of attention from my parents. What about you?"

"My mom was busy supporting us, so I spent a lot

of time alone. But that was okay," he said quickly. "I'd lose myself in a book."

"Where did you grow up? City or country?"

"In Chicago. They have a great transportation system so I could go to the Field Museum, the planetarium or the movies anytime I wanted. And I'd go down to Navy Pier, along the lakefront. It's so big it feels like an ocean. What about you?"

"We lived in Ellicott City, outside Baltimore. I was in the suburbs so I couldn't go anywhere on my own. If I wanted to go to the mall or the movies, my mom had to drive me." She dragged in a breath and let it out in a rush. "It's getting easy to talk to you. I'm usually cautious with men."

"Why?"

"That ghost incident years ago made me realize how easily people can turn on you."

"You felt attacked?"

"I felt like people didn't want to believe it, so they turned it around on me."

"Then I'm honored that you let me get close."

"Honored?"

"Does that sound too stiff?"

She grinned. "It sounds old-fashioned."

He grinned back at her, letting his happiness bloom in the confines of the car. He wished he could totally relax, but he couldn't banish a nagging worry that his original purpose for coming to Jenkins Cove was going to blow up in his face.

Sometime very soon, he was going to have to fess up. But not yet.

Instead, he asked, "Did you sense something strange in the warehouse?"

"Did you?" she shot back.

He felt his jaw clenching, but he managed to say, "Yes."

"What?"

"I can't describe it. The feeling of the air being thick with menace. The feeling of a presence there that I couldn't define."

"Yes," she answered. "It was something like that. But not exactly menace. I felt like there were spirits in the building, and they wanted my help."

"I guess that's the difference between you and me. They think they can reach you."

"So you believe?"

"I didn't before I came to Jenkins Cove."

"Of course, my aunt does. That's why she has the psychomanteum. To help people. That's how she is. She's generous."

"So are you. Do you think she was a big influence on you?"

"I always admired her." She turned toward him. "What influenced you?"

He struggled for an answer. "I learned early that you have to be responsible for yourself. I think that made me goal-oriented. And maybe rigid."

"Do you wish you were different?"

She was giving him an opportunity to come clean with her. But he couldn't take it. Not yet. "Sometimes. What about you?"

She swallowed. "I'd like to be more open with people. I'm working on it."

Perhaps neither one of them wanted to reveal any more. They rode in silence for a few minutes. Then Michael said, "I guess we'd better agree on what we're going to tell Chief Hammer."

"What do you have in mind?"

"We stick as closely as possible to the truth. Your aunt suggested that we go look at the warehouse because I was interested in local history. Someone was watching us. When I ran after him, I fell into a covered pit."

"Local history," she said in a low voice. "Okay."

He reached over and placed his hand over hers. "It's not exactly a fib."

"But it's not what she really said. I've always felt better about sticking to the truth."

"Yeah," he answered, inwardly wincing. He'd feel better about it, too. But he'd trapped himself.

He sat in silence beside her as they drove to the police station, knowing her tension was increasing as they approached.

"One more thing before we get there. I've been thinking about who might have a reason to—" He stopped and then started again. "Harm you."

She sucked in a sharp breath. "Why would anyone want to harm me?"

"Well, there's the obvious—the murder. If the guy thinks you can identify him, he might come after you."

"I can't!"

"Maybe he doesn't know that."

She took her lower lip between her teeth. "I guess it won't do any good to take out an ad in the paper."

"Unfortunately, no." He turned to her. "Let's talk about that real-estate guy—Ned Perry."

"Ned? What about him?"

"Well, he's trying to convince your aunt to sell a piece of prime property right on the harbor. But your aunt still wants to run the B & B—which she can't do without you."

Chelsea made a strangled sound. "Do you think he'd really go after me?"

"You're in his way. But I don't know how far he'd go to remove an obstacle."

She gave him a worried look. "You're not planning to say anything to Chief Hammer about it, are you? I mean, it's just a suspicion."

"No. But I'll keep an eye on Ned. And maybe I can find out where he was this afternoon."

He heard her swallow.

"You know," she said in a strangled voice, "a couple of times I thought maybe someone was lurking around the house."

"Yeah?"

She shrugged. "I never saw anyone. It was just a feeling that I was being watched. So I don't want to say that to the chief, either."

"You're sure?"

"Yes."

"How well do you know Phil Cardon?" he asked.

"Why?"

"He came into the Duck Blind right after I did the other night. He sat next to me at the counter and wanted to get into a big conversation. He could have followed me back and tried to run me down."

"I always thought he was harmless."

"Okay," he answered, but he'd keep the guy on his suspect list.

Ten minutes later, they arrived at the police station. Chief Hammer was at his desk. Michael could understand Chelsea's concerns as soon as he met the smug, overconfident man. Toward Chelsea, he was highly condescending.

Apparently he was the kind of bozo who responded better to other men, so Michael took over the interview, telling about how he'd tried to follow the guy watching them.

"You didn't have to go after him," the chief said.

"I wanted to know what he was doing there."

"That could have been dangerous."

"It turned out to be," Michael answered. "Somebody dug a hole in the ground and covered it up. I fell in."

The chief inspected him. "You get hurt?"

"Not much."

"Well, it was probably kids fooling around," Hammer answered.

"Maybe," Michael allowed. "But we'd be remiss if we didn't report it to you."

"Thanks for stopping by," the chief answered.

Michael clenched his fists at his sides. Was Hammer going to investigate? He stopped himself from asking the question.

When they stepped into the sunshine again, he muttered, "It's good to get a breath of fresh air."

Chelsea gave him a sidewise glance. "So it's not just me being paranoid about the chief."

"No. Now let's go back and tell your aunt it was an interesting experience."

"Okay," she answered in a small voice.

Once again, he could feel her tension growing as they rode back to the House of the Seven Gables.

When they got out of the car, he came around to her side and slung his arm around her. She turned toward him, and he pulled her against him.

"I'm not used to depending on anyone else," she whispered.

"Neither am I."

"Guys aren't expected to depend on people," she answered.

Aunt Sophie chose that moment to come outside.

Chelsea took a quick step away from Michael, her gaze fixed on the boats in the harbor.

"I see it was a successful trip," her aunt said.

Michael swallowed. "Yes."

"So, what did you think about the warehouse?" Sophie asked.

"It was atmospheric," he answered.

"Long ago, indentured servants were brought to the Colonies. Some of them came through Jenkins Cove. They came here under horrible conditions. Not much better than the way slaves from Africa were transported."

Chelsea gasped. "I never knew that." Her gaze shot to her aunt. "You're not saying that warehouse is over two hundred years old, are you?"

"No. That building is newer. But it's constructed on the location of one of the old docks." Sophie put a hand on her niece's arm. "Some of those people died soon after they arrived. You're sensitive. I think you sense their agony."

Michael felt a shiver go up his spine.

Chelsea stared at her aunt. "How do you know about the slaves and the indentured servants?"

"I did some research at the historical society."

Chelsea's gaze turned inquisitive. "Why didn't you tell me any of that?"

"Years ago, when you saw that ghost, you were too young. But that's why I sent you to the warehouse. And sent you with Michael, in case you had any problems."

He shifted his weight from one foot to the other and winced.

Chelsea's gaze flew to him. "Your knee. You've been standing here all this time."

"What about his knee?" Sophie asked.

Chelsea looked as though she was searching for an explanation.

Michael did it for her. "I tripped when I was out there by the warehouse."

"Yes. I told him he should put some ice on it."

"A good idea."

They all went into the house.

"You sit down," Chelsea ordered, gesturing toward the living room.

He sat, and so did Sophie.

Quickly Chelsea returned with a freezer pack wrapped in a dish towel. He put it on his knee and leaned back.

Chelsea stood regarding him for a minute. "There are more ice packs in the freezer if you need another one."

"Thanks."

She reached out her hand and let it drop back. "You took some pictures. Can I see them?"

"Sure." He pulled out the camera, then tried to turn it on. Nothing happened. "Damn."

"What?"

"I must have broken it when I fell."

She nodded. "That's too bad."

"Yeah," he agreed. He'd wanted to see what kind of effects he got in the warehouse. Now that wasn't going to happen.

Chelsea looked toward the hall, then back again. "I have things to do."

"Sure."

When Chelsea had left, Sophie murmured, "She's sensitive. Don't hurt her."

Maybe the older woman didn't want to hear his answer, because she got up and walked into the kitchen, leaving Michael sitting in the living room, feeling a sudden chill as if a cloud had slid across the sun.

Chapter Nine

"You don't have any other guests?" Michael asked Sophie the next day, when he was the only one who showed up for breakfast.

"We turned down some bookings because we're getting ready for the town Christmas party. It's going to be here this year. And you're invited."

"You're sure I'm not in the way?"

"Of course not. We've got a lot of jobs for a man—if you're game."

"Of course."

"Come help me rearrange some furniture in the living room so we'll be ready for the Christmas tree."

He dutifully moved the sofa and one of the chairs.

"We're hoping that Brandon and Clifford Drake can come to the party," Aunt Sophie said as she stood back to see how the arrangement looked.

"You mean the local squires?" he teased her.

"Something like that." She handed him a feather duster. "You're tall. Can you make sure the top of the wall molding is free of cobwebs?"

His mother had made him do a lot of household chores, and he'd sworn that he would never do them again. At home in D.C., he had a maid who came once a week. But he did as Sophie asked; he liked her and he wanted to help.

Over the next few days, he saw that the party gave Chelsea the perfect excuse to avoid him. She was helping her aunt get ready for one of the premier Jenkins Cove events of the holiday season. But he needed to speak to her, and when he saw the opportunity to corner her in the kitchen, he took it.

The kitchen. That room had connotations he'd like to avoid. But she was there, and he wasn't going to miss the chance to talk to her.

She was standing at the stove, stirring a large pot of something that smelled wonderful and listening to Christmas music on a CD player. She looked wonderful, too, even if she appeared a bit frazzled.

When she looked up and saw him, her hand froze.

"How have you been?" he asked.

"Okay."

"I've been worried about you."

"I'm fine!" She gave him a critical look. "How's your knee?"

"Much better."

He wanted to close the distance between them, turn her around and pull her into his arms. Instead, he kept his hands at his sides.

"You told me you'd seen someone lurking around the house. Then there was that guy out at the warehouse. Have you seen anything else suspicious?"

"No."

"You'd tell me if anything worried you."

"Yes."

The way she said it held the sound of dismissal, but he stayed where he was. "You and I need to talk."

"I know. But I'm so focused on the party now. It's going to have to wait until after that."

In response, he walked across the room and turned off the burner, then lifted the spoon out of her hand.

She stared at him, wide-eyed. "What are you doing?"

"This." He pulled her into his arms.

"Michael, don't."

He kept saying things—doing things—that surprised him. This was no exception. "Just for a minute. I need to hold you for a minute."

He'd tried to stay away from her, but now, when he lowered his mouth to hers, the familiar heat flared between them.

She didn't resist him. As soon as their lips touched, she was kissing him back with all the passion he remembered.

"Thank God," he murmured against her mouth. "I thought you were avoiding me."

"I was," she answered, still kissing him.

He sipped from her, nibbled at her, pushed them

both to a level of arousal that he knew was a mistake. There was nothing they could do about it now. He couldn't carry her away from the stove and into his bedroom. Or—

He laughed softly.

"What?" she murmured.

He lifted his mouth from hers and said, "I was picturing myself dragging you into the pantry and making love to you against the shelves."

"Oh!"

"But when I make love to you for the first time, it's going to be in a nice comfortable bed," he added, then pressed his mouth more firmly to hers again, stroking his hands over her back and shoulders, then lower so that he could pull her hips against him.

He was so far gone that his brain had stopped functioning. He wanted her and he couldn't get the bed image out of his mind. What if he really did take her back to his room and do what they both wanted so much?

Then he heard the doorbell ring. Moments later, footsteps sounded in the hall.

Chelsea sprang away from him, smoothing her hair, then turning on the burner again with a jerky motion and starting to stir with such vigor that spicy sauce slopped out onto the stove.

Twenty seconds later, the door opened, and Sophie bustled in with a large, flat box in her hand.

"Cookies for the party," she said, then saw that Chelsea wasn't alone.

"Why, Michael," she said, "what are you doing here?"

"I was just leaving."

"Have one of Mildred's blond brownies. They're famous in Jenkins Cove."

"They can't be more famous than your own," he managed.

Aunt Sophie flushed with pleasure.

Michael grabbed a brownie and made a hasty exit from the kitchen, thinking that in another minute he would have had Chelsea's blouse off. And then what would Sophie have thought?

Well, it would only be confirmation of what she already suspected. At least the fooling around part. The question was, did she suspect why he'd come to the House of the Seven Gables?

No, she couldn't. If she had, she wouldn't have been so hospitable.

He ate the brownie as he hurried back to his room. Grabbing his coat, he exited the B & B. The day before, he'd spent a lot of time at the Maritime Museum, poking into the history of the town, and he'd bought some books about the area at the museum's gift shop and at some of the other shops in town.

Now he climbed in his car and headed for the warehouse where he and Chelsea had gone two days ago.

THE WATCHER STAYED IN THE shadows of the shed down by the dock. Maybe this was the opportunity he'd been waiting for. Bryant was leaving. Which left the two women in the house alone—since they hadn't booked any other guests for the rest of the week.

From where he stood, he had a good view of the kitchen through two big windows. He could see Chelsea standing at the counter beside the sink—working on party preparations, he assumed.

The aunt marched in, pulled a sheet off the magnetized notepad stuck to the refrigerator and started taking notes. It looked as though she was going to the grocery store—for a ton of stuff, judging from the amount she was writing.

Perfect!

Now all he had to do was wait for Chelsea to leave the kitchen for a few minutes and he could have some fun with her. Well, more than fun, he hoped. Maybe he could get rid of her this morning.

THIS TIME MICHAEL HAD NO problem finding the access road to the warehouse on his own.

He drove up the narrow lane, keeping his eyes peeled for trouble. Once again, there appeared to be no one around, but this time he wished he was carrying a gun.

Though he didn't have a permit for one, he hated feeling exposed.

After getting out of the car, he rolled back the

warehouse doors on their rusty hinges and stepped into the cavernous space, feeling the familiar twinge of uneasiness.

As they had the last time, a flock of seabirds took flight, getting out of his way as he strode to his left and stood against the wall. The birds were gone, but it still felt as if the place was occupied.

He might have said the building was haunted. By the ghosts of indentured servants who had died in Jenkins Cove?

He didn't want to put it in those terms. He'd settle for saying that the warehouse gave him the willies.

Gritting his teeth, he ignored the prickling at the back of his neck as he looked around and realized something was different from the day before.

Last time he and Chelsea had been here, debris had littered the floor. Now it looked as though someone had swept the place clean, except for the bird droppings that had collected along the walls.

Had the police been here? Surely they wouldn't have swept up.

So who had felt compelled to clean the floor? And why? Those were interesting questions.

Maybe the guy who'd been here was using the building for something illegal. Smuggling, perhaps. Would Hammer blow that theory off, too?

In any case, the building gave off bad vibes, and he wanted to step outside into the sunshine again. He forced himself to stay inside, listening.

He could hear the wind whistling through the cracks in the walls. As he strained his ears, it seemed to change in tone—to a sound more like people screaming.

Screaming?

He shuddered and heard himself say, "Stop."

There was no reason for the wind to obey him, but the sound changed again. This time it was like voices whispering Chelsea's name.

He pressed his hands over his face, fighting to keep his equilibrium. If he stayed here much longer, he would go insane.

Teeth clenched, he walked to the door. Still, he knew it was dangerous to simply walk outside again. Last time someone else had been here. Forcing himself to hang back in the shadows, he scanned the parking area and the woods.

Apparently, nobody had followed him from town. Suddenly that was not reassuring.

If the person who was lurking around wasn't watching him, then he was watching Chelsea.

That was why the voices had called her name.

He shook his head. The analysis didn't make perfect sense. Still, he couldn't fight the urgent feeling that he had to get back to the House of the Seven Gables.

He raced back to his car, jumped in and headed toward Jenkins Cove, blowing the speed limit to hell.

When he pulled into the lot across from the B & B, he saw that Aunt Sophie's car was missing. She must be out. As he started toward the house, he thought he saw someone dart behind the side of a shed down by the harbor.

Was that the person Chelsea had seen watching the house?

He took off at a run toward the shed, but by the time he reached the area, he saw no one.

Then a roaring sound made him whirl.

A boat starting up.

Charging onto the dock, he saw a small motor-boat with a low canopy top rapidly pulling into the harbor. The driver was hidden by the canopy.

He cursed under his breath. He'd come back to town because he was worried about Chelsea—and he'd let himself be lured away to the dock.

Turning, he trotted back to the house.

He'd covered about half the distance when he heard Chelsea scream.

Fear leaped inside him, and he started running flat out.

In seconds he was at the back door. Throwing it open, he bolted into the kitchen, which was where the scream had come from.

Chelsea was standing by the sink, looking dazed.

"What happened?" he shouted as he ran toward her, almost slipping on the wet floor. Regaining his balance, he took her in his arms.

Her lips moved, but instead of answering, she gave him a confused look.

Being careful not to slip again, he scooped her up, then carried her to one of the kitchen chairs, where he sat down and cradled her in his lap. She had started to shake.

"What happened?" he asked again. "Take a breath and tell me."

She gulped in air and let it out again. "I turned on the blender and I got a bad shock," she whispered.

His curse rang through the kitchen.

"The blender," she said again, in a strangled voice. He stared at the machine, which sat on the counter, the glass bowl full of lumpy pink and white ingredients. Then his gaze shot to the water on the floor again. "You could have gotten killed!"

Her lips trembled, and he wrapped his arms around her, rocking her gently, silently thanking God that the shock hadn't been worse.

Her right hand was curled into a loose fist. He uncurled it and pressed it to his lips.

It could have been an accident. But the way things were going, he wouldn't bet on it.

"Were you out of the kitchen before it happened?" he asked.

"Why is that important?"

"Just answer the question."

"Yes. I went up to the bathroom."

"And then you came back and turned on the blender?"

She nodded. "I was going to make a salmon spread for the party."

"Was the floor wet when you left the kitchen?"

"The floor?" Her gaze shot to the puddle of water on the tile. "Where did that come from?"

"I'd like to know."

He turned so he could look at the door—which he'd left open. "The door was unlocked?"

"It usually is during the day."

"So someone could have come in here and put the water on the floor. I guess you were damn lucky that the ground fault interrupter tripped."

Her breath caught. "Who would do that?"

"Good question."

"Maybe there was a leak from the sink," she murmured.

"I don't see the puddle getting bigger," he pointed out.

He stroked his hands over her back and shoulders. "Have you had trouble with the blender before?"

"It was okay the last time I used it."

"Which was when?"

"Yesterday."

He might have gotten up, strode to the blender and emptied the contents into the sink, but he couldn't turn Chelsea loose yet.

As he winnowed his fingers through her hair, she lowered her head to his shoulder and clasped her arms around him.

"You think someone came in here while I was out of the room?" she whispered.

"I don't know. I saw someone outside."

She gasped. "Where?"

"Over by the dock."

"That's not exactly in our yard. It could have been anyone."

"They took off in a boat when I went over there."

"Still…"

"From now on, I'm going to stay around the house." Her head jerked up. "I don't need a babysitter!"

"I wasn't suggesting you did."

"Then what?"

"I want to make sure you're safe."

She answered with a small nod, then cleared her throat. "And are we going to call Chief Hammer?" Her voice turned edgy as she asked the question.

"Do you want to tell him about this?"

"No! We can't prove anything."

"There could be fingerprints."

"You don't think someone who would come in here to…do mischief would be careful about something like that?"

"You're probably right," he conceded.

THE MAN WHO HAD TAKEN OFF in the boat slowed the craft and lifted a pair of binoculars to his eyes. This little scenario wasn't working the way he'd expected.

There was Chelsea in the kitchen, sitting on Bryant's lap. He'd expected her to drop to the floor, electricity coursing through her body because he'd crossed the wires in the old metal blender. But the circuit breaker had tripped or something and turned off the damn power. Saving her life.

Too bad, because she was still a problem that needed to be solved. Of course, the guy who'd hired him was getting a little worried about how things were going. But the watcher was on top of it. If the boss wasn't going to take drastic measures, somebody needed to do it for him.

His thoughts were interrupted by a car pulling up in the parking area near the B & B. Aunt Sophie returning from the grocery store. Well, maybe it was time to head across the harbor before one of them spotted him.

A NOISE AT THE BACK DOOR made both Michael and Chelsea start.

"Who left this door wide open?"

Aunt Sophie walked into the room, holding two bags of groceries. Her gaze shot to the couple sitting on the kitchen chair.

"Well!" she said. "Pardon me for barging in."

Chelsea leaped up, then started to speak rapidly. "I had an accident. Michael heard me scream, and he came in to find out what happened."

"And what did happen?" Sophie asked.

"The blender gave Chelsea a bad shock."

Her aunt gasped. "Are you all right?"

"Yes."

Michael cleared his throat. "Have you ever had anyone coming into the house making trouble for you?"

She stared at him as if he'd asked her if she'd recently taken a rocket ship to Mars. "Of course not. Why are you asking?"

"Because there was water on the kitchen floor and Chelsea didn't spill any."

As he spoke, Chelsea knelt down, opened the cabinet below the sink and felt inside.

"It's dry," she murmured.

"You haven't seen anyone lurking around here?" Michael pressed.

The older woman's face wrinkled. "Sometimes we get kids making mischief. Once I had some boys throw eggs at the front door."

Chelsea winced. "You never told me about that."

"It only happened once—a few years ago."

"But nobody's come in and done anything in the house?"

"Not that I know about," she said.

"Well, I think it might be a good idea to keep the doors locked," Michael said.

"Young man, I operate a bed-and-breakfast. How can I possibly keep the doors locked?"

"You give your guests keys," he said. "Like you do when they come back after hours."

"You give out a bunch of keys, and someone's going to lose one," Sophie objected. "And if I do it, people will think we've got security problems in town."

"Possibly. But I hope you'll consider taking that precaution."

"I will. But you're the only guest here now," she pointed out.

"I can take a key to a locksmith and get some made for you," Michael offered.

Sophie's expression changed. "You're serious about this."

"Very serious."

Chelsea sighed, then walked to a drawer and took out a key and handed it to him. "I'll go to the locksmith with you."

He'd been hoping she'd say that, but he hadn't wanted to be the one to suggest it.

"Let's clean up first," she said. She started sopping up the water with paper towels.

Michael pulled the plug on the blender cord in one quick motion. Then he turned the blender over and examined the bottom. It looked as though someone might have fooled with the casing, but he couldn't be sure because he didn't know the condition of the appliance.

When Chelsea walked back to the counter and reached for the blender, he saw her hand was shaking. But she lifted off the glass container and emptied the contents into a mixing bowl, which she put into the refrigerator.

Then she grabbed her coat. "We'll bring in the groceries," she told her aunt.

When they'd transferred the groceries to the house, they stepped outside again.

"I'm not used to being stalked," she said.

"That makes two of us."

"But it looks like they're after me."

"I'm the one who almost got hit by a car."

"Yes. But it still could have been an accident."

"You believe that?"

"I don't know!" She kept her face turned toward the harbor, but she gave him a sidewise look. "Show me where the guy was standing and where his boat was moored."

Chapter Ten

Chelsea felt her throat tighten as they walked toward the harbor area. When Michael reached for her hand, she jumped. "Don't."

"Why not?"

"People will know there's something between us."

His voice took on an intimate warmth. "I want them to know."

Chelsea could not manage a reply.

They walked the rest of the way, holding hands. She wasn't used to anything like that, but she told herself to relax. He was putting his mark on her. It was a strange sensation, yet she couldn't deny that she liked it.

Still, she warned herself not to like it too much. What would happen when he left Jenkins Cove? She shoved that thought to the side and let him lead her to the place where he'd seen someone watching the house.

"This is the shed," he said, pointing to the small wooden building. "Who owns it?"

"The company that takes tourists on little cruises up and down Jenkins Creek. They own a boat that's in dry dock now. They use the shed for storage. But this is the off-season, and it's not running."

"So anybody could have been around here." He walked to the shed and rattled the door. It was unlocked. Stepping inside, he looked around. He saw some folding chairs, some life preservers and some packages of plastic cups. In the middle of the floor was a crumpled brochure. He stooped to pick it up, then stepped outside into the sunlight and smoothed it out.

Chelsea looked over his shoulder. "It's one of those maps that the chamber of commerce gives out. They distribute thousands of them every year."

"But look at this." He tapped his finger on the map. "Some of the landmarks are circled. Like your house, for example." He slipped the map into his pocket.

He walked around the building, looking at the ground. Along one side was a bald spot in the grass, where someone could have been standing. Or maybe the spot had been there since the summer, and nobody had gotten around to putting in a patch of sod.

"Where's the boat slip?" she asked. "Where you saw him take off?"

He led her onto the dock, then a few yards farther along. "You know who this belongs to?"

"It's one of the slips tourists can use. But most people don't come here by boat at this time of year."

"So we still don't know anything."

"Sorry."

He cleared his throat. "You didn't have any problems in town—until you ran across that man assaulting a woman in the swamp?"

"Well, there was the old ghost story."

"Yeah."

"I should get back to work," she said, changing the subject.

"We were going to get keys made. And you could take a lunch break."

"I already grabbed some leftovers."

"I can get some takeout and bring it back to the house."

"There's still some quiche. Unless you think real men don't eat quiche."

"I ate it for breakfast," he pointed out. "Where's the locksmith?"

"Just across Main Street."

"Okay, I'll take you up on the lunch offer, if you walk there with me."

She nodded.

They walked down to the locksmith, where she ordered six keys. Then he stopped at the coffee shop that was right on the corner of Center Street. Although he looked casual as he stood in line to order, she was getting to know him, and she saw that he was watching the people.

"You're wondering who did it?" she murmured.

"Yeah."

"If they left in a boat, they probably aren't still here."

"Unless they came back."

She gave him a quick glance. "I just can't think of Jenkins Cove like that."

He lowered his voice. "We have to go back to the main event. The murder was real."

"Yes."

Neither one of them mentioned the ghost on the road. Was that real, too? She had wanted to dismiss ghosts from her life. It seemed she wasn't allowed to do that.

After he bought his coffee, they walked back to the House of the Seven Gables, where she heated a slice of quiche in the microwave and set out a basket of muffins.

Probably they should be continuing the discussion about the blender and whether someone had come into the house, but she was distracted. The party was a big deal, and she wanted it to come off well, not only because of Aunt Sophie but because she had something to prove to the town—that she could fit in here.

MICHAEL NOTED that the activity at the House of the Seven Gables got more frantic as the day and hour of the party drew near. Not only were Chelsea and Sophie cooking and cleaning, but they were decorating the house for the holiday.

A curvy brunette with gray eyes delivered boxes of garlands for the fireplace mantels. Chelsea introduced her as Lexie Thornton, a local landscape designer who was selling Christmas greenery for the holiday season.

But the garlands were far from the major decorations in the public areas of the B & B. Crystal bowls of shiny glass balls, teddy bears wearing holiday outfits and ornamental nutcracker soldiers were set around on tables.

Chelsea's painting of Main Street occupied a place of honor over the living room mantel. On a nearby table was a dual roll of tickets and a box where people could pay ten dollars a chance to win the painting. The proceeds were earmarked for town improvements.

Michael managed to get out of the house to take the blender to a repairman who operated out of his home a few miles from town. But he had a lot of backlog, and he said he couldn't check out the appliance until later in the week.

The night before the party, Phil Cardon delivered a huge fir tree, which he set up in the living room. Michael watched him closely, but Cardon seemed only interested in doing his job, getting paid and leaving.

Michael, Chelsea and Aunt Sophie stayed up until well after midnight decorating the tree with strings of miniature white lights and antique ornaments.

The next day, when Chelsea sent Michael out for

an emergency carton of sour cream and eight ounces of cream cheese, he was glad to escape from the frantic preparations.

After all that work, he expected Chelsea to look frazzled. But when she came downstairs just before five on Thursday in a floor-length green satin dress that hugged her curves and set off her pale skin and blond hair, he almost forgot to breathe.

"You look spectacular," he told her.

She slid her gaze over his black slacks, blue shirt and tweed sports jacket. "So do you."

"Should I put on a tie? I didn't know it was such a fancy affair."

Aunt Sophie came bustling in from the kitchen with a tray of cookies, which she set on the lace-covered table in the dining room. She was wearing a bright red skirt and a creamy blouse with frills down the front. Studded through the folds of lace were tiny lights that blinked on and off. It put her in competition with the Christmas tree.

"Some people dress up more than others," she said to Michael. "Dr. Janecek and some of the other men will probably come in tuxedos. And Phil will wear a work shirt and jeans."

"Who's Dr. Janecek?"

"A physician in town."

"Clifford Drake usually wears a tuxedo, too."

The guests started arriving around five. Or rather, the suspects, as Michael thought of them. He wanted a chance to meet these people and see how they interacted with the two Caldwell women.

In the next twenty-five minutes, the B & B filled up with guests. As advertised, a man came in wearing a tuxedo. He was slim and had dark brown hair with silver wings. His eyes were also dark.

"Clifford Drake or Dr. Janecek?" Michael asked Chelsea.

"Clifford."

A few moments later, another tuxedoed man joined the crowd. He was slender and balding, which he had tried to disguise by combing long strands of hair to the side. His lips were thin, and his dark eyes were deep set.

"The doctor?" Michael asked.

"Yes."

One of the women immediately cornered him, and Michael supposed from his expression that he was being asked for free medical advice.

Another man came in wearing a three-piece suit with a watch hanging from a chain. He looked a little nervous, and Michael was immediately on the alert.

He leaned toward Chelsea. "Who's that?"

"Edwin Leonard, the butler at Brandon Drake's house."

"Is he upset about something?"

"He does look a little on edge," Chelsea whispered.

When Leonard spotted Sophie, his eyes lit up, and he crossed the room toward her.

"He's been here before," Chelsea said. "I think he's sweet on Aunt Sophie. And the feeling is mutual."

They went over, and Chelsea made the introductions.

"Is Brandon coming?" Sophie asked eagerly. "It's been such a long time since we've seen him in town."

"I'm afraid he decided to stay home once again," Edwin answered. "But he practically ordered me to come to the party and have a good time."

"It's too bad he wouldn't come himself."

The butler shook his head. "He's still grieving for Charlotte. I suggested that he might talk to her through the psychomanteum, but he doesn't want to try it."

Michael listened, nonplussed. It was strange to be hearing a perfectly normal conversation, then hear mention of the psychomanteum.

Sensing spirits in the old warehouse was one thing. Going into a darkened room and inviting them to communicate with you was quite another.

"Poor man. Maybe you can change his mind," Sophie murmured.

"There are some other people I'd like you to meet," Chelsea said.

Michael took the hint. Chelsea was giving her aunt and Edwin Leonard a chance to be together.

As she led him through the crowd, he heard someone clear his throat. Turning, Michael saw the doctor.

"We haven't met."

"Dr. Janecek, this is Michael Bryant," Chelsea said.

In answer to the doctor's inquiring look, she added, "Michael is spending some time with us at the House of the Seven Gables."

"Did he come down here to use the psychomanteum?" the doctor asked.

"No," Michael answered. "I'm just taking a few days to enjoy Jenkins Cove."

"I'm glad you don't believe in that claptrap," Janecek said.

Michael saw Chelsea's jaw tighten, but she didn't come back with a denial. When he saw her glance across the room, he spotted Chief Hammer talking to some of the Main Street merchants, while he ate from a paper plate of cookies and other goodies that he'd gotten off the buffet table.

The chief spotted Chelsea and nodded. She nodded back but stayed on her own side of the room.

Michael watched Ned Perry sidle up to her.

"Have you talked some sense into your aunt?" he asked.

"If you mean about selling the House of the Seven Gables, I have no intention of doing that."

"You're making a mistake," he said in a tight voice.

"I don't think so."

Michael watched the exchange with interest. He hadn't liked Perry on their first meeting, and the man was making himself even more unpleasant. Could he have been the one who'd been following them around? Or what if he'd hired some-one to do it?

And what if Ned was willing to go even further? What if he'd hired someone to come into the house and spread that water on the floor?

Michael moved Ned Perry to the top of his suspect list, then wondered if he was jumping to convenient conclusions. He wanted a solution, so he was manufacturing one.

Once again, he checked to see what Chelsea was doing and found her talking to one of the Main Street merchants.

At the beginning of the party, she'd seemed to be having a good time. Now she looked a little distracted, as though she were listening to voices other people couldn't hear. That thought set his nerves tingling.

He wanted to ask her what was wrong, but he couldn't really do it now.

He saw other people he recognized. The garden center owner, Lexie Thornton, had come in and was talking with Rufus Shea. There seemed to be some-thing between them.

"They know each other pretty well," Michael commented to Aunt Sophie.

"Lexie used to date Rufus's son, Simon."

"The guy who died."

"We presume he's dead. He disappeared thirteen years ago."

Michael watched the parade of guests. People

from all strata of Jenkins Cove society seemed to be mixing and mingling. On the surface, they appeared to get along, although Michael suspected that there were probably some truces that had been called for the holidays.

Still, the party was a success. It was close to midnight by the time the house was finally cleared—except for Edwin Leonard, the butler from Drake House.

Sophie went to a box on a table near the fireplace and looked through the cash and tickets there.

"We collected almost five hundred dollars for the town fund," she announced.

"That's fantastic," Edwin said. He added, "Let me help you clean up."

"I don't want to put you to any trouble," Sophie answered.

"No trouble. I'm an expert at it."

"Of course."

True to his word, Edwin was excellent at cleaning up. He organized the four of them into teams. Michael and Chelsea carried food into the kitchen. Sophie and Edwin put it away.

Then they all tackled the plates and cups that guests had left around the house. Sophie and Leonard went out onto the back porch.

Chelsea turned to Michael. "You were a big help, too. Thank you."

As they walked into the hall, he thought this

might be his chance to ask her what had happened at the party to disturb her. She looked so worn-out that he only said, "You go to bed. I know you've got to be exhausted."

She nodded and started toward the steps. But something about the set of her shoulders told him that she wasn't headed for bed.

So what was she up to?

He hung back, then followed her to the second floor, where he was pretty sure her bedroom was located. Instead of stopping, she climbed the steps to the third floor.

She couldn't be going to work in her studio, could she? Not after such an exhausting day. And not in her party dress.

He caught his breath as he saw her turn the other way down the hall from her studio. When she opened the door to the psychomanteum, his heart started to pound.

CHELSEA TURNED ON THE DIM overhead lights and closed the door behind her. She'd always resisted coming into this room.

But after Edwin had mentioned it during the party, her thoughts had kept coming back here.

Edwin was a levelheaded man. If he thought that Brandon Drake could contact his dead wife, then maybe there was something to it. But it wasn't just Edwin's suggestion that had sent her up here.

She shuddered. In the warehouse, she'd had the sensation that a spirit was trying to speak to her. She'd told herself then she was just letting her imagination run away with her.

Tonight, however, the feeling was even stronger, and she knew she was just going to lie in her bed, tossing and turning, until she came here and tried to make contact.

She shuddered again.

She didn't *want* to make contact. She just wanted to be left alone. Apparently that wasn't an option.

She picked up the lighter on one of the tables and walked around the room, lighting the candles. Then she turned off the overhead lamp and sat down.

She wasn't even sure what to do besides stare at her own reflection in the mirror. She appeared ghostly in the flickering light.

Maybe she should have changed out of her party dress. But she'd wanted to get this over with and had rushed up here. Now she was stuck.

If you were uncomfortable, she wondered, did that make it harder or easier to communicate with the dead?

Whichever it was, she was going to sit here and wait—even if she spent the night in this room.

What a thought!

She had been dead tired. Now she was wide-awake because all her senses tingled with anticipation.

She wasn't sure how long she sat staring into the

mirror. She wanted to look at her watch, but that seemed like too much of a modern intrusion when the room harked back to ancient times.

After a while, the flickering candlelight and the late hour made her want to close her eyes. But if she did that, she wouldn't be able to see the mirror, and that was part of the process, wasn't it? Too bad she hadn't paid more attention to how this place worked.

Realizing her hands were clenched in her lap, she tried to relax them. But she needed someone to hold on to, and she was the only one here.

Or was she? Goose bumps suddenly covered her bare arms as she stared into the mirror. She was the only person who had walked into the room, and yet she thought she saw another figure—a woman—standing in back of her.

Her breath caught as the figure became more real, more solid. No, maybe *solid* was the wrong word. Though she could see the woman standing there, she could still see right through her.

As the back of her neck prickled, the urge to turn around assaulted her. She fought it.

"Did you come to talk to me?" she whispered, hardly expecting an answer.

"Yes," a voice answered, so close that she imagined she could feel the woman's breath on her neck.

Not warm breath. Cold.

She gasped, and it took every ounce of willpower

she possessed to keep herself from jumping up and dashing out the door. But she stayed where she was.

"Chelsea Caldwell," the woman said in a high, strained voice that seemed to come from everywhere and nowhere.

"Yes." Chelsea kept her gaze fixed on the mirror, watching the ghostly shape beside her. The figure looked like a woman wearing a translucent veil that covered her from head to toe.

"You must help me." The woman spoke in a thick accent that made it hard to understand her.

"How can I do that?"

"You must bring us justice."

Chelsea raised her hand pleadingly, gesturing toward her own reflection. "But…I don't know how."

"You must go back to that place where you saw the murder! Near it. Near the pine tree that has half its branches burned away on one side."

"What do you mean?"

"You will know when you see it. Go to the place where you saw me murdered."

Chelsea gasped. "You? That was you?"

"Yes."

Gathering her courage, Chelsea asked the question that had been deviling her since the incident on the road. "I saw you lying on the road. Then I saw someone murder you. How is that possible?"

"The first woman was not me. It was another one

who died here. Long ago. She came from the same country as I did."

"What country is that?"

"It is far away. It had a different name when she lived there. That is not the important part. She and I are not the only ones. Many people have come to this charming little town as we did. Some with hope in their hearts and some with despair. But they had one thing in common. They died. They are buried in a mass grave. You must help the police find them."

Chelsea's throat had gone so tight that she could barely drag in enough air to speak. "Why…are you asking this of me?" she managed to ask.

"Because you are sensitive to us."

"No."

"My name is Lavinia. Remember my name."

The way the woman spoke and the directness of her contact sent a shiver up Chelsea's spine. Still, she protested. "I have no idea where to look for this grave."

"I told you. Near the spot where you saw me murdered. Look for the tree. And do not deny your abilities. You have powers you have never wanted to recognize. That is why I can reach out to you. No one else. It happened when you were a girl, didn't it? But you weren't ready."

Chelsea gasped. "Who was that first woman?"

"Another one of us."

As the woman spoke, she raised a ghostly hand, a hand still shrouded by the veil.

When she came closer, Chelsea huddled away from the advancing form. "Don't," she whispered.

Ignoring her, the woman touched Chelsea's cheek, sending a dart of icy cold onto her skin and through her body.

Unable to help herself, she cried out.

Chapter Eleven

Michael threw the door open and sprinted into the psychomanteum.

He felt a whoosh, as though a vacuum had suddenly opened in the enclosed space, pulling air out of the room and into some other place.

Last time he'd been here, the ceiling light had illuminated the room. Now it was lit by dozens of flickering candles. Chelsea sat on the chair in the center of the floor, facing the ornate mirror.

When the door opened, she leaped up and whirled toward him, wavering on her feet.

"Michael?" she gasped.

He rushed around the chair and caught her in his arms the way he had after the blender had shocked her. In the dim light, she looked much as she had then.

Shocked. But this time it wasn't because of electricity.

"You have to get out of here," he said, recognizing the urgency as he spoke the words.

When she opened her mouth, no sound came out. Scooping her into his arms, he cradled her against his chest as he strode out of the room.

"The candles," she murmured. "You can't leave the candles burning."

"Damn." He turned back toward the room, and his breath caught in his throat. The candles had gone out, as though someone had walked through the room, extinguishing them the moment they had left.

That was impossible. Yet he had seen it with his own eyes.

He might have puzzled on that longer, if not for Chelsea. She hooked her arm around his neck and pressed her cheek to his chest.

"I'll take care of you," he murmured as he carried her downstairs to the second floor. "Which is your bedroom?"

Without hesitation, she answered, "At the end of the hall. In the right-hand wing. The family wing."

He strode past the guest area, to a doorway that closed off the end of the hall.

Once he had turned to shut that door, she murmured, "First room on the right."

She leaned over, turning the knob, and he carried her into a bedroom that was furnished much like the guest rooms in the house—with lovingly restored antiques. Only, this room was filled with personality.

Her possessions were arranged on the tables and dresser. Little ornaments like a Japanese good luck cat. Family photos. A bookcase along one wall was brimming with art books and paperbacks.

He laid her on the bed, and when he tried to straighten, she kept her arms around his neck.

"Don't go. Hold me," she whispered.

He wasn't sure that was such a good idea, but he understood that she needed him at that moment. In truth, he couldn't resist the invitation. He kicked off his loafers and eased onto the bed beside her.

She sighed. "Thank you."

She turned her head, staring at something, and he followed her gaze to find she was looking out the window into the darkness.

"You see something?"

"No. That's the trouble," she said, as though she were totally confounded by the lack of light outside. "So I can't do it now."

"Do what?"

"Find the mass grave."

He winced, feeling as though he'd come in in the middle of the conversation. "What are you talking about?"

She gave him a quizzical look, apparently realizing that she'd left out a few details.

"Something happened to you in that room. What was it?" he demanded.

She kept her gaze fixed on his face as she swallowed hard. "A ghost came to me."

He swore under his breath, then apologized. "Are you sure?"

"Yes. I felt someone calling me during the party, and I knew that I had to go up there. I knew that something was going to happen in that room."

"Is that why you got that strange look on your face?"

"Yes. After Edwin started talking about the psychomanteum, I knew I had to go in there." She gulped. "It was like a...force tugging at me. It turned out to be a ghost. She said her name was Lavinia."

"She gave you her name?"

"Yes." She raised her head so she could give him a direct look. "You don't believe me."

"You believe it. That's good enough for me," he said. "But I wasn't there, so I don't know what happened."

"She wanted me to know about a mass grave. But it's too dark to find it now."

"Yeah."

She kept her gaze fixed on him. "I have to do it first thing in the morning. Will you come with me?"

"Of course."

"Thank you." She tightened her grip on him, and he shifted her body so that she was cradled against him.

He'd fantasized about lying with her in a bed. He'd even talked to her about it. And he wanted her now.

When she nuzzled her lips against his neck, he was pretty sure she was thinking the same thing.

Before she could tell him she wanted to make love, he raised his head. "We're both dead tired."

"Yes."

He stroked his lips against her cheek, then said, "Which makes the timing pretty bad right now."

She heaved in a breath and let it out. "Are you making excuses?"

"No. I'm being realistic. But there's the other side of the equation, too. The idea of leaving you when you've had a frightening experience makes my stomach knot. I want to hold you for a little while. Will you let me stay?"

The warmth in her eyes almost broke his resolve not to do more than hold her.

"Yes." She turned off the light on the bedside table.

He settled down beside her, gathering her close, staring down at her breasts, wanting to cup them through the silk of her dress. He knew that if he went that far, though, he would throw good intentions out the window. Instead he contented himself with stroking her arms and shoulders, soothing her with his hands and words. He felt the tension in her, yet his touch seemed to help her relax. It worked for him, too.

He closed his eyes, letting himself drift, feeling the mattress below him and Chelsea in his arms. With his eyes closed, he could focus on the wonderful scent of her and the soft sound of her breathing.

When he opened his eyes again, he was shocked to see that it was no longer dark. Faint light was coming in through the window. When he shifted slightly, her eyes blinked open. For a moment he guessed that she didn't know why he was in bed with her.

Then comprehension dawned.

"Last night, I talked to Lavinia in the psychomanteum. Now I have to go out to the bog to look for the grave," she whispered.

"Now?"

"Yes."

"Aren't you going to help your aunt finish cleaning up?"

She shook her head. "There's someone coming in from town to help. That was part of the deal when we agreed to have the party here."

"Okay." He got out of bed and scuffed his feet into his loafers. It had been a while since he'd slept in his clothes, and he wanted to take a shower and change, but he wasn't going to insist on it.

She also got up. When she looked down at the green party dress she was still wearing, she made a face. "I can't go out to the swamp like this. And if I'm going to change, then I might as well shower."

"Okay. I'll meet you downstairs in half an hour."

He left her room and tiptoed down the stairs. Before he reached the bottom, Aunt Sophie walked across the front hall, carrying a tray full of paper plates and napkins that were left over from the party.

She stopped and looked at him.

"It's not what you think," he said.

"Oh?" She kept her gaze fixed on him. "Come down the rest of the way, so you don't tower over me."

Obediently, he descended to the first floor.

"Chelsea went into the psychomanteum last night. A—" He stopped short and started again. "A spirit contacted her, and she was upset. I stayed with her, in her room, and we both fell asleep."

"Uh-huh."

Speaking quickly, he went on. "The spirit wanted her to do something. To go look for a mass grave. She wants to do it as soon as possible, so we're both changing our clothes and going out."

"Search for a mass grave," Sophie repeated in a soft voice. "A spirit asked Chelsea to do that?"

"Yes."

She gave him a long look. "You think you'll find it?"

"I don't know," he answered honestly. "But I'm not letting Chelsea go out there by herself."

"Thank you."

"I need to take a quick shower and change first."

"And I'll fix you something to eat."

"I don't think Chelsea wants to take the time."

"We'll see about that," Sophie answered, heading off toward the kitchen.

Michael hurried down the hall to his room, thinking that some mighty strange things had happened to him since coming to Jenkins Cove.

And the conversation he'd just had with Aunt Sophie was one of the strangest. She'd taken it for granted that Chelsea's encounter with the ghost had been real. Now she was making sure her niece had a good breakfast before going off to follow the spirit's instructions.

He took a shower in record time, then dragged a razor over his face and brushed his teeth before putting on clothes and the waterproof hiking boots he'd bought at one of the shops in town.

By the time he returned to the kitchen, Chelsea and Sophie were both there, speaking in low voices. They both looked toward the door as he walked in.

Her aunt spoke up in a firm voice. "I've persuaded Chelsea that the grave's not going away. There's no point in skipping breakfast."

Chelsea answered with a little nod, then accepted a cup of steaming coffee from her aunt.

"I'll make you bacon and eggs," she said as she brought Michael coffee.

"I don't want that much," Chelsea objected. "Besides, we have all those cookies and quick breads from last night."

Sophie gave her a disapproving look. "That's not a very nourishing breakfast."

"In this case, it's going to have to do."

Chelsea retrieved the plate of pumpkin bread and a tin of cookies.

"My kind of breakfast," Michael said as he helped

himself to a spice cookie. But he could tell Chelsea was in a hurry, so he didn't allow himself to linger.

They were out of the house a few minutes later.

"I'll drive," Chelsea said.

"I'm not used to being driven around," he shot back. "What's your excuse this time?"

"The same as last time. I know where we're going, and you don't."

He watched her expression turn grim as they climbed into the car. He wanted to tell her that she didn't have to do this—just because a ghost had given her an assignment. He knew it wasn't strictly true, though. Chelsea had to do it.

They turned right on Main Street and drove toward Tilghman Island. A few miles outside town, she slowed, and he saw her looking for something.

"This is the same location where they found the body?" he asked.

"Near here. The body was a little farther up that way." She gestured. "I use that sign as a marker."

He wanted to point out that he could have headed for the sign, but he saw the tension on her face as she pulled onto the shoulder.

"You have some other landmark?" he asked.

"Yes." She peered around, apparently searching for something, and pointed to a tall, misshapen pine that looked as though it had been struck by lightning. "The ghost told me to look for a tree that had its branches burned off on one side. That must be it."

"Okay."

A car drove slowly past. The driver looked at them, but didn't stop.

"Was that Phil Cardon?" Michael asked.

"Yes."

"I wonder what he's doing out here."

"He probably had a job."

Or he followed us, Michael thought.

Chelsea opened her purse and took out a small revolver. Michael gaped at her. "You have a gun?"

"Yes. For protection."

"And you have a permit to carry?"

She made a face. "No. But I'm going to do it anyway."

They both climbed out of the car and stood on the gravel shoulder, where she slung the strap of her purse over her shoulder.

She looked around. "I haven't been back here since…that night. But now that I see it in the daylight, I remember this place. A friend used to have a fishing cabin about a half mile from here. Her father would take us out there."

"Where do you want to start looking?"

"Let's head toward the tree."

"All right." Michael reached for her free hand and clasped her fingers tightly as they started walking into the swampy area. There were cattails and scrubby bushes and low trees that he didn't recognize. Though most of them were leafless in the winter, some still had foliage—either broad-leaved or pine.

Mud sucked at their boots, making it hard to walk as they tramped farther from the road. Michael kept his gaze on the ground, unsure of what he was looking for. Probably not a white cross sticking out of the muck.

When they came out onto slightly higher ground, he breathed out a little sigh. With the mud no longer trying to pull his boots off, the walking was easier, yet he felt a coldness in the air, like the first night when he'd walked from the House of the Seven Gables to Main Street.

Beside him, Chelsea raised her head, looked around and made a small sound, and he wondered if she was feeling the same thing.

"This place is spooky. I think I'd go home if I were alone."

"Safety in numbers."

She swung toward him. "Not just anyone would do," she said in a low voice.

He felt his heart leap. Instead of speaking, he slung his arm around her shoulder.

She turned in a small circle. "I wish the ghost had been more specific. I don't know where to start looking."

He wanted to be supportive, even though he had little faith in a ghost's orders. "Follow your instincts."

She sighed. "Maybe I had a hallucination last night."

"Do you mean you wish you did?"

"Yes," she whispered, and once again, her honesty tore at him. She wasn't making up stories about ghosts. Something had happened, and she obviously didn't know how to handle it.

She started walking again, and he stayed close beside her.

After about five minutes, he spotted something that wasn't natural to the landscape. Something grayish-white, half buried in the ground.

He pointed. "Over there."

When they came closer, he stifled a spurt of disappointment. It was only a tennis shoe.

"Anybody could have lost that," she murmured, echoing his thoughts. "Maybe that's its mate over there."

She pointed to another object about the same color. But when they came closer, he caught his breath. The shape wasn't much like a shoe.

"I think this is something a little more significant." He found a stick he could use to dig. Squatting down beside the grayish-white lump on the ground, he began to carefully scrape the dirt away.

As the shape emerged, Chelsea gasped. "It's a skull," she whispered. "A human skull, not some animal who died out here."

"Yes, it is."

"So this *could* be a mass grave. What should we do?"

"I think we'd better leave the skull here and see if we can find anything else."

"Okay."

They kept tramping across the ground, both of them looking down. When Chelsea made a small sound and pointed to her right, Michael hurried over. This time they saw a long bone—like part of an arm.

"Either this is a graveyard, or animals scattered some bones," Michael muttered.

He had just started off to search some more when he was stopped by the sound of a small explosion and something whizzing past his head.

Lunging back, he caught Chelsea's hand and tugged her toward the ground.

Chapter Twelve

Chelsea gasped as Michael pulled her down.

Turning her head, she stared at him. "Someone took a shot at us?"

"Yeah."

She made a strangled sound, trying to wrap her head around what was happening. "Who would do that?"

He brought his mouth close to her ear. "Keep your voice down. It's someone who doesn't want us to get out of here and report what we've found."

As he spoke, it happened again. The small explosion and then the sound of something whizzing past them.

Chelsea's heart skipped a beat, then started up again in double time, and she had to clench her jaw to keep from crying out. Somehow when she'd bought her gun and practiced at a firing range, she hadn't imagined someone shooting back at her.

"They didn't even warn us," she whispered.

"I think that's the idea."

His words made her picture two more bodies in the swamp—Michael's and hers—and she shuddered.

He clasped her shoulder.

"It's going to be okay," he whispered.

Was it?

"Give me the gun."

She handed it over. Michael moved along the ground, so that his body was covering hers, shielding her.

"Stay down," he whispered.

They huddled in the bushes, and no more shots sounded.

"Where are they?" Chelsea whispered. "And what are they going to do?"

"I'd like to know. If we're lucky, we can get back to the car and get out of here. Can you follow me?"

"Yes," she answered, because she didn't see any alternative. They couldn't stay out here like sitting ducks. And what good did a gun do them if they couldn't see who was shooting at them?

Hysterical laughter threatened to break through her terror. Or maybe it was because of the terror. Sitting ducks. A lot of people shot at ducks in this part of the country. She'd never thought she would be like the water fowl.

Michael began crawling across the ground, using a clump of bushes as a screen. As he moved, he circled around, heading back toward the road. They had covered about thirty feet when she heard four more shots, rapid-fire.

"It's not near us," Michael whispered as he reached back to put a hand on her arm. "Quiet."

She did as he said, and she heard a whooshing sound. "What is it?"

"I think that's air escaping from your tires."

She struggled not to gasp.

"So we can't drive away," he clarified. "We've got to go the other way. Come on."

Michael started moving farther into the underbrush, staying low to the ground. Chelsea followed as fast as she could. It was a hard way to travel, and she wasn't sure how long she could keep it up.

But she had to. If she didn't, whoever was out there would find them.

She wanted to look behind her, but she knew that would only slow her down and expose her face. Instead, she kept crawling.

They traveled through the underbrush, stopping every few yards to listen. They were heading toward the bay. She knew that much. Beyond that, she didn't have a clue.

What would they do if they came to the creek? Plunge into the frigid water or turn along the bank? Neither seemed like a good alternative.

As she kept moving, it felt as if the air was thickening around her, the way it had in the psychomanteum.

Something made her look up. Ahead of her, she saw the air waver. Then, to her astonishment, she saw the figure of a woman.

When she made a strangled sound, Michael turned. "What?"

"Up there."

He looked where she was pointing, then shook his head. "What?" he said again.

"You don't see her?"

"I don't see anything."

"It's the ghost. Lavinia."

He closed his eyes for a moment, then opened them again, and she wondered if he thought the stress had driven her around the bend.

The ghost gestured, then spoke in a low whisper. "This way. Hurry."

Chelsea caught the urgency in her voice. She crawled past Michael, following the ghost because that seemed to be her only option.

As she moved, her hand and then her knee hit something solid, something different from the springy vegetation that they had been crawling over. A series of wooden boards.

She stopped short, and Michael came up beside her. "What?"

"There's something here." She gestured urgently toward the boards.

He moved to the side and pulled the solid surface. Like a door, it opened to reveal a hole in the ground.

"It's like the pit at the warehouse," he muttered. "Only it's designed to keep someone out—not make them fall in."

He pushed the door up just enough so that he could slip inside, then reached his hand up. "Come on."

She didn't like going into a hole in the ground. If the person stalking them found them down there, they were trapped. But if they stayed out here in the open, the gunman would likely gain on them, because they couldn't make much headway crawling.

Michael seemed to think it was the best alternative, which gave her the guts to climb down into the hole.

She slipped under the cover, squeezing through, scraping the top of her hand before dropping a few feet to the ground below.

She winced.

"What happened?"

"My hand. It's just a scrape."

He cursed. "Sorry."

"I'm fine," she said, even though her hand was throbbing.

"What is this place?" he whispered.

"Maybe smugglers used it. Or it could be from the underground railroad."

"That was over a hundred and fifty years ago." After a second he added, "We'd better not talk."

"Okay."

It was almost pitch-black inside the hole. She wouldn't use the small flashlight in her purse; it might shine out through the cracks in the boards. Then, to her astonishment, an eerie blue glow rose in one corner of the space.

She gasped and jumped back. If there wasn't someone outside with a gun, she would have scrambled back out of the hole in a heartbeat.

"What the hell?" Michael muttered, taking a step back, his whole body poised to fight some unknown enemy.

"You see it?" she whispered.

"Yes."

As she stared at the blue light, a strange sensation stole over her. The light had startled her initially, but now she felt a kind of friendly feeling emanating from it.

Michael tried to shove her behind him, but she put a hand on his arm. "It's okay. I think the ghost is lighting this place for us."

Even to her own ears, that sounded ridiculous. At the moment, though, that was the only explanation she could come up with.

"Yeah, well, the ghost is going to get us caught," he muttered.

The light flickered for a moment, then steadied.

"We'd better use it," she whispered as she began to inspect their refuge.

It was a pit about six feet deep and five feet square. In the blue light, she could see a wooden wall at one side. Crossing the dirt floor, she pulled at the wall, and it swung aside, revealing another, smaller space.

"We need to get in there," she whispered.

Michael looked doubtfully at the tiny crevice.

His hesitation made her stomach knot. "Please. Just do it. And hurry."

He turned to stare at her, then did as she asked, climbing in, then reaching for her.

She squeezed into the narrow passage after him, pulling the wall back into place. There was hardly any room, so that they had to huddle together.

As they did, she heard a sound—footsteps walking through the underbrush above them.

She felt Michael's body stiffen and knew he had raised the gun. In the darkness, she clung to him.

Was the blue light still shining in the main chamber? Would it give them away?

And would her breathing? It seemed to ring in her ears, to fill the whole enclosure with sound.

She kept repeating a silent prayer. *Keep walking. Just go on by us. You don't know we're here.*

Whoever was searching the area above them didn't seem to get the message. He stopped walking, and she waited for him to pull the door back.

Instead, from above, she heard another volley of gunshots, coming in rapid succession, this time blasting through the wooden planks and into the hole. Four, five, six shots.

She cringed.

Then there was a scraping sound, and she realized the gunman was pulling the boards aside.

Would he figure out where they'd gone? That they were in the hole, hidden from view by the door at the side of the pit?

Breath frozen in her lungs, she waited and she felt Michael tense, ready to shoot.

Long seconds passed, and her body grew stiff from holding the same position. But she dared not move.

Finally, whoever was up there muttered a curse—presumably because he thought the hole was empty and he didn't know where they had gone.

After what felt like an eternity, he dropped the wooden cover back into place with a bang. Again, centuries ticked by before she heard his footsteps recede.

Michael brought his mouth to her ear again and spoke in a barely audible voice. "We have to stay here for a while."

"How long?"

"I don't know. Until he gives up looking for us and leaves."

She nodded against his shoulder. "Can we get out into the main pit?"

"Better not. He could come back and decide we doubled back and hid in here."

"Okay." She shifted a little, trying to get more comfortable.

He reached up to touch the ceiling above them,

then the walls. Keeping his voice low, he said, "I think we can stretch out our legs. If we hear him coming back, we'll pull our legs in and move the door back into place."

"Okay."

He moved the door aside, then slid his legs forward, making a sound of satisfaction as he shifted out of the cramped position. She did the same. "What a relief."

He gripped her arm. "Keep your voice low. If he hears us, we're dead."

"We have a gun."

"A revolver. And he's got an automatic weapon. Unless we can set up some kind of ambush, he's got too much of an advantage."

She dragged in a breath that sounded more like a moan.

"Sorry."

"No. You're right," she answered in a barely audible voice. "And he's probably still out there looking for us."

As they both contemplated that unhappy truth, Michael asked, "I don't suppose you have a cell phone?"

"Sorry. I left it in the car. What about you?"

"I'm not getting enough bars in the area, so I left it in my room." He sighed. "That was a serious miscalculation."

"Neither one of us thought we were going to get shot at."

"So why did you bring a gun?"

"I guess I've been…worried."

"Since I came here?"

"Before that." She swallowed. "I kept feeling like someone was watching me." Raising her head, she looked upward. "So, who do you think it was up there?"

"I wish I knew. We have to assume it's somebody involved in the murder. He followed us out here."

"We saw Phil Cardon drive past."

"Do you have any reason to believe he might be a killer?"

Chelsea thought about it. "I can't say I like him a lot, but I also can't picture him killing that woman. Lavinia."

The mention of the ghost brought her back to the way they'd found this hole in the ground.

"She helped us find this place." She turned her head toward Michael, although she couldn't see him in the dark. "Do you believe that's true?"

She heard him drag in a breath and let it out. "I guess I have to. I can't come up with any other explanation for your finding the hole or for that weird blue light."

"Yes."

He gripped her hand. "There's something I should say to you."

The way his voice sounded in the darkness made her stomach knot. "What?"

"When I came here, I thought the whole ghost business was…" His voice trailed off.

"A bunch of crap?" she asked, unable to keep an edge out of her own voice.

He sighed. "You could put it that way."

"Everybody was talking about me."

"Yeah."

She wanted to ask him more questions, but a sound from above made them both go rigid.

Footsteps? Was the guy coming back, looking for them?

Quietly, Michael drew his feet back into the hole. Chelsea did the same, then reached for the wooden wall and pulled it back against the opening to the little tunnel. Michael shifted again so that he was cradling her and yet still holding the gun in firing position. He pressed his lips to her cheek, and she closed her eyes, huddling with him in the dark, wishing she could pretend they were in bed together and not a hideyhole in the ground.

The footsteps passed by, not right beside the hole but a few feet away. Either the guy wasn't going to look in the hole again or he'd forgotten the location. Neither meant he was giving up.

Michael shifted so that he could look at his watch. It was after nine. If they planned to wait until cover of darkness, they had a long wait.

Above them, thunder sounded, shaking the ground nearby.

Then rain began to pour down.

She could hear it pattering on the wooden boards that covered the top of the hole.

It pounded steadily, and when the ground underneath them grew wet, Chelsea grimaced. Pushing the wooden wall aside, she saw rain pouring into the hole.

"Maybe this was a safe hiding place when we first came down here," Michael muttered. "But it's not safe now. We've got to get out of here."

She felt her throat tighten. "What if the guy is still up there?"

"Maybe he thinks the storm will do us in."

It could, she thought, but she didn't say it aloud.

"I'll go up and have a look," Michael said.

She grabbed his arm. "No!"

"If we stay down here, we're going to drown in mud," he said. "So unless you have a better suggestion, I'm going topside."

Chapter Thirteen

While Chelsea waited in the dark, wet hole, Michael stretched up and eased the cover aside. As weak daylight and rain flooded in, she braced for the sound of shots. Luckily all she heard was the rain pounding down and splashing into the water at the bottom of the pit.

Michael heaved himself up and flopped onto the ground. Again, she waited for shots. Again there was only the rain—and another clap of thunder.

Long seconds ticked by until Michael finally reached down for her. Clasping his fingers around her forearm, he tugged her up, and she slithered onto the ground.

"Stay low," he warned as he started crawling through the underbrush.

She followed him, moving awkwardly, praying that they got out of the area without being spotted.

They were fifty yards from the pit when he stopped behind a clump of scrubby trees.

Chelsea pulled up beside him. Her coat and pants were soaking by now, and she knew they had to find shelter.

"Did you say there was a hunting cabin around here?" he asked.

"Yes."

"Do you remember where?"

"No. But maybe I can find it." She looked around, trying to orient herself. She hadn't been to the cabin in years, but she remembered it was closer to town than where they'd stopped the car.

"Can we stand up?" she asked Michael.

"I hope so," he answered, getting to his feet and looking around.

Cold rain pelted down, and now it was mixed with sleet. If they didn't get inside soon, they were going to be in big trouble.

She pulled up the hood of her coat, grateful for the shelter it gave her. Glancing at Michael, she saw water running through his hair and dripping down his face.

When he saw her expression, he pulled her close and gave her a quick, hard kiss.

"More later," he promised, then wrapped his arm around her waist as they made their way through the scrubby landscape, both of them stepping into water-filled holes from time to time as they floundered onward.

Chelsea's teeth chattered. Her hands had started to feel like blocks of ice, and she could barely put one leg in front of the other. With the part of her brain that was still functioning, she fought panic, because she was pretty sure that she had missed the cabin.

"I have to stop," she whispered.

"No. You have to keep going," Michael answered, holding her up as they staggered onward.

When she was about to drop in her tracks, she did a double take. A building loomed ahead of them in the gloom—a building she hadn't even seen until she was almost on top of it. At first she thought she had made it up, as she took several wavery steps forward, but it stayed real and solid. It wasn't the hunting cabin. It was someone's summer home.

"There." She gestured with as much strength as she could muster.

They approached the door and climbed wide front steps. Reaching out a hand that looked half-frozen, Michael rang the doorbell. When no one answered, he tried to turn the knob. She almost sobbed when it didn't open.

Plopping down on the steps, she sat with her teeth chattering, looking out at the rain and sleet falling around them.

They were so close to shelter, yet it might as well be a million miles away.

Michael began searching along the edge of the steps. Several flowerpots had been grouped in an arrangement near the door. He picked them up, then held up his hand triumphantly, showing her a key.

When he'd opened the door, he hauled her up and into a foyer.

There she sat down on a bench, waiting while Michael walked down the hall, her brain too numb to take in much—other than the reality that they were finally sheltered from the storm.

Leaning her head against the wall, she closed her eyes for a moment. She wasn't sure how long she sat there. But she opened her eyes abruptly when Michael laid a hand on her shoulder.

"Come on."

"Where?"

"To the bathroom."

He led her down the hall to a white marble bathroom. She looked down at their muddy footprints. "We're making a mess."

"We'll clean up later."

He tugged off her wet coat, then started working on her wet pants. Next he sat her down on the closed toilet seat and helped her out of her boots.

When she was wearing only her damp underwear, he helped her into the bathtub, where he dipped a cloth in a small pot of warm water and washed off her hands and face.

"Where did that come from?" she asked in confusion.

"The hot water is turned off, but there's a propane tank for the stove. I heated a little water."

When she was cleaned up, he led her down the

hall to a bedroom, then pulled aside the covers. It was cold in the bed, but her body heat and the wool blankets he'd piled on began to warm the sheets.

A few minutes later, Michael came back and slipped in beside her.

She sighed as he rubbed his hands up and down her arms and over her back and shoulders.

"That feels good," Chelsea murmured.

"I'm glad."

"I wish we could turn on the heat."

"That's not working. Neither is the phone, unfortunately. We're lucky there's propane in the tank."

"Can he find us here?" she whispered.

"I think he gave up the hunt when the rain started."

"But you don't know for sure."

"He'd have to plunge into the bush to find us. This house is an unlikely spot to take refuge. And if he tries to get in, we've got a better chance here than in that hole. So your job is to get some rest. Then we'll find our way back to town."

She moved closer to him.

A little while ago she'd been so cold that she could barely think. Now she was warming up. As her body returned to normal, she couldn't help noticing Michael's muscular leg against her. His broad shoulders. His narrow hips. And the erection pressed to her middle. She ducked her head away from him and grinned.

He'd told her more than once that it wasn't the

right time to make love. Now, though, she had him trapped in a bed—and she meant to make the most of the opportunity.

"Are you feeling better?" he asked.

"Yes. And I think you are, too." She raised her face to look at him as she slid her hand down his body and cupped the bulge at the front of his shorts.

His exclamation sounded like a mixture of surprise and need. "Don't."

"Why not? Are you going to tell me this is the wrong time and the wrong place? Again?"

"I should."

"I have a better suggestion. Give in to what we both want."

She rocked her hand against him, marveling at her own audacity but loving the wonderful feel of him.

She'd never been the aggressor in lovemaking. But now she was going to get what she wanted.

When Michael's mouth came down on hers for a hot, hungry kiss, she knew that she had wiped away his doubts.

At least for now.

She'd settle for that—and figure out the rest later.

The storm still raged outside. Inside the vacation house, another kind of storm seethed.

When he covered her mouth with his, she opened for him, telling him with her lips and body and hands how much she wanted him.

His kiss was greedy. The greed itself gave her as

much pleasure as the physical sensation of his mouth moving over hers.

Heat coursed through her as he strung small kisses over her cheeks, her jaw, her neck and then lower, to the tops of her breasts.

Reaching around her, he unhooked her bra, pulling it off and out of the way as he ducked under the covers so that he could nuzzle his face against her breasts, kissing first one inner curve and then the other.

"So good," he whispered.

"Yes," she answered, cupping the back of his head and holding him to her as he took one hardened nipple into his mouth and sucked.

The pleasure was exquisite. It doubled as he took its mate between his thumb and finger, imitating the action of his mouth.

He rolled to his side, taking her with him so that they were facing each other on the bed.

His gaze locked with hers as he slid his hands over her back and shoulders, pressing her breasts to his hair-roughened chest, then slipping lower to cup her bottom and seal her more tightly to his erection as he rocked her in his arms, creating an exquisite friction between them.

She played her fingers over his shoulders, down his back, loving the feel of his body. Boldly, she slipped her hands into the back of his shorts, cupping his buttocks, massaging him there.

"I love the way you feel," she whispered.

"Likewise."

He slid his hand between them, into her panties, dipping into her most intimate flesh, stroking her in a way that raised the level of her arousal to fever pitch.

"You're so hot and wet for me," he growled.

"Yes." She pulled down her panties and kicked them down her legs before tugging at his shorts. He helped her get rid of his underwear, then angled her body so that he could stroke her cleft with his erection.

She caught her breath as he bent his head, sucking at her nipple again.

The pleasure was exquisite, and she couldn't hold back a sobbing sound.

"I want you inside me," she gasped. "Now."

She rolled to her back and opened her legs. He followed her over, covering her body with his, and she guided him to her.

As he entered her, he brought his mouth back to hers, his kiss hot and tender at the same time.

Then he raised his head, looking down at her.

She met his gaze, marveling that this was finally happening.

He held still for several long seconds; then, when she was about to beg him to move, he did, setting up a steady rhythm.

He built her tension, holding back his own need for release until she was poised on the brink of climax.

Only then did he increase the tempo, sliding his

hand between them to press against her core as he pushed her up and over the final rise.

She soared to the top of a high peak, then toppled over the edge, sobbing his name as rapture took her. As incredible pleasure rolled over her, she felt him follow her.

Spent, he collapsed on top of her, and they both lay breathing hard and fast.

When he tried to move off her, she clasped him to her. "Stay here."

"I'm too heavy."

"No. I like the feel of you on top of me."

She turned her head to slide her lips against his neck.

Circling her shoulders with his arms, he pulled her against himself and rolled to his side, still joined to her.

She snuggled against him, trying to absorb the reality of this moment. She had known him only a few days, yet nothing else in her life had ever felt so right.

"You should sleep," he murmured.

"You, too."

"Someone has to keep guard."

She winced. He'd transported her from the real world into a place where only the two of them existed. But that was only an illusion. Someone had tried to kill them, and he was still out there somewhere.

She hitched in a breath. "We have to get back to town."

"Not in this storm."

"Maybe there's a car in the garage."

"Maybe. But we don't have the keys. Starting cars without them isn't one of my talents."

"Too bad."

MICHAEL STROKED his hands over Chelsea's hair and shoulders, then pressed a light kiss to her cheek.

"Sleep," he said again, willing her to relax. It was heavenly to lie next to her, to hold her in his arms. Heavenly to have made love with her. Yet at the same time, so many worries swirled in his head that it was impossible for him to relax.

Someone was still stalking them. He didn't know who it was or if he was going to come crashing in the door. But Michael vowed to keep Chelsea safe.

He lay there holding her for another few minutes, listening to the sound of her even breathing. Then he eased away from her, careful not to wake her up.

Outside the warm bed, he shivered. Picking up the gun from where he'd left it on the bedside table, he went exploring through the house. It was small. There was only one bedroom, with a large closet. Obviously, a married couple with no kids came down here in the summer months. Maybe for long weekends.

In the closet he found both men's and women's clothing. He pulled on jeans that were two inches too short and a sweatshirt.

He couldn't find jeans that looked as though they'd fit Chelsea, but he figured men's sweatpants would do. And another sweatshirt. He laid them on the end of the bed, then went to the bathroom and found their wet hiking boots, which he put into the oven on low heat. Hopefully, they'd dry out in a few hours.

The refrigerator was off, and open, but he found some food in the pantry. A box of crackers. Some canned soup, which he could heat on the stove.

He looked out the window. It had stopped raining, and that worried him. With the weather cleared up, the guy who had tried to kill them could resume his search. Hopefully this was an unlikely place for him to look. Michael could now see that the house was part of a small community of summer houses.

He pictured himself going out and knocking on the doors of the other houses. Then he changed his mind. From this vantage point, it looked as though nobody was home.

He stepped out, inspecting the walkway leading to the front door. The rain had washed away their muddy footprints, so that didn't give them away.

Hopefully, they were safe here for a few hours, but he wanted to get back to town soon and report the shooting incident to Chief Hammer. There was no way the chief could ignore the bullet holes in the boards. Or could he?

He'd just stepped back into the hall when a noise in back of him made him draw the gun and whirl.

When he saw Chelsea standing a few feet away

with a shocked expression on her face, he shoved the gun into the waistband of his jeans. "Sorry. I guess I'm a little jumpy."

She nodded. "We both are."

He saw that she'd dressed in the clothing he'd laid out for her.

"Where are my shoes?"

"In the oven. I couldn't find any in the closet that fit you. What are you doing up?"

"I guess I couldn't sleep."

"Then we should eat something and get out of here. I found soup and crackers."

"We're already making a mess of these people's house."

"We can leave them a note—telling them where to get in touch with us. And we can clean up later. Maybe they'd like a free couple of nights at the House of the Seven Gables."

"Right."

They went into the kitchen. While he fixed some chicken noodle soup, she wrote a note. Then they sat down and quickly ate the simple meal.

When Chelsea started to rinse the bowls under cold water, she winced.

"What's wrong?"

"My hand." She held it up, and he could see that the place where she'd scraped herself had reddened.

He crossed to her and held the wound up to the

light coming in the window. "It looks like it's getting infected. You'd better have the doctor look at it."

She answered with a tight nod.

He returned to the bathroom and picked up their coats.

Chelsea followed him. "They're still wet."

"We'll leave them here and borrow some."

"I don't like to do that."

"I know. But it's safer. If we're dressed in clothing he doesn't recognize, that may make the difference between getting back to town safely and not."

She made a disgusted sound. "You keep thinking of things I don't."

"You're not used to evading killers."

"Are you?"

"No. But my devious mind comes up with unpleasant scenarios and offers solutions."

"What about my car?"

"We'll get a tow truck to haul it back later."

"My registration is in there."

"Yeah. But whoever was shooting at us already knows who we are."

"Thanks for reminding me."

They hung the wet coats in the attached garage and wiped the mud off the hall floor. Then they ripped off the sheets and put them in the laundry room.

Back in the closet he found two light rain jackets. Neither was very warm, but they each put on another sweatshirt underneath. The jackets had hoods, which would help disguise their appearance.

And he found a woman's scarf, which Chelsea used to partially hide her face.

By the time they were ready to leave the house, it was almost three in the afternoon.

He was praying it was safe to head back to town. Still, he felt a shiver go through him as they stepped outside and closed the door behind them.

He replaced the key that he'd found under the flowerpot. "Do you know where we are in relationship to the highway?" he asked.

She looked around, then pointed to an access road. "I think we'll find it if we go that way."

"Okay."

As they started off down the long drive, he kept checking their surroundings, alert for anyone suspicious.

They reached the highway, just as a police car with flashing lights came speeding toward them.

It screeched to a halt, and a young officer jumped out. "Police. Freeze. Hands in the air."

Chapter Fourteen

Michael cursed under his breath, but he raised his hands. Beside him he could see Chelsea do the same thing.

At the same time, she called out, "Officer Draper. It's Chelsea Caldwell and Michael Bryant. Why are you holding a gun on us?"

"Chelsea?" the cop asked. "Okay, take off that hood. But don't make any funny moves."

Chelsea shoved the hood back, then unwound the scarf, revealing her face.

"It's you, all right," the officer muttered. "What are you doing breaking into a house?"

"You know about that?" she gasped.

"Yeah." He looked from her to Michael. "One of the neighbors saw you come outside a while ago."

"I thought nobody was home," Michael told him, "or I would have asked for help."

"Explain what's going on."

He nodded, then asked, "Can I put my hands down?"

"Keep them where I can see them."

Michael did as instructed, hoping the guy wasn't going to pat him down and find the gun.

"We were out near the site where Chelsea saw that woman killed, and somebody started shooting at us," he said.

Officer Draper stared at him. "Uh-huh."

"Well, we can show you the fresh bullet holes in the boards above the hole where we hid."

"Okay."

"We left a note in the house where we were inside," Chelsea said. "I left my name and number so the people could get in touch with us. We can show you that, too."

Draper nodded.

Michael cleared his throat. "We were out at the site of the shooting, because…" He stopped, wondering how he was going to put the next part.

"Because what?" Draper demanded.

"Because we had information that there was a mass grave out there."

Draper's eyes narrowed. "Information from where?"

Beside him, he could hear Chelsea drag in a sharp breath.

"From an old diary," Michael said, lying through his teeth.

"Oh yeah?"

"Chief Hammer will want to have a look around

there. We found a human skull. There are probably other bones. We think that's why whoever it was shot at us. He didn't want anyone poking around the grave."

Draper's stance had changed. "Let's go back there and have a look," he said, watching them carefully.

"Sure," Michael said. After the initial shock of almost getting arrested, he had started to realize this was the best thing that could have happened to them. If someone was trying to kill them, he was unlikely to do it in the presence of a cop.

"First, I want to see that note you said you left in the house," Draper said.

Michael wanted to yell at him that the graves and the bullet holes were a lot more important than the interior of the house, but he forced himself not to object. Instead, he waited while the patrolman made a call to his chief. Then they went along quietly, Michael holding his tongue as the cop inspected the condition of the house. From this vantage point, he was glad that Chelsea had left that very apologetic note.

After Draper had wasted enough time at the house, they headed for the highway.

When they reached the location of their ordeal, they found Chief Hammer waiting for them. He was looking at Chelsea's tires.

"You see the bullet holes?" Michael asked.

"Yeah. Who shot at you?"

"I'd like to know."

"Show me the pit where you hid."

Michael glanced at Chelsea. "You want to stay here?"

"I want to come with you."

They all tramped back into the swampy area, and for a while, Michael's stomach clenched when they had trouble locating the pit.

Too bad Lavinia didn't appear to guide them again.

No, scratch that.

Finally they found it by themselves.

He stood with his arm around Chelsea as Hammer inspected the bullet holes. "It looks like you were damn lucky. How did you find this place?"

Chelsea cleared her throat. "I used to play around here when I was a kid," she said.

Apparently she had decided that if Michael could lie, she could, too. No, he silently amended. She *had* played around here; she just wasn't prepared to tell him how she'd actually discovered the pit.

"We found the skull over there," Chelsea said, pointing to the approximate location. But when they led the cops back there, the evidence was missing.

"My guess is that the killer took it away," Michael was quick to add. "If you keep looking, you'll probably find more bones."

Hammer made a noncommittal sound.

So, what was wrong with this guy? Michael wondered. For a cop, he didn't seem much interested in evidence of murder. Was he lazy? Incompetent? Or did he have something to hide?

"Can you recommend a company to tow my car?" Chelsea asked.

Hammer gave her the name of a local garage.

"And there's the question of who shot at us," Michael said.

"There's that."

"Are you going to report it to the state police? It sounds like it's part of the murder case."

"Mmm-hmm," Hammer said, without really answering the question.

"Chelsea could be in danger," Michael added. "The killer may think she knows something. But we're actually both clueless."

The chief turned to her. "Maybe you want to get out of town for a few days."

Michael wanted to ask what good that would do if the chief wasn't going to solve the crime, but again he held his tongue.

As they started back toward the road, Michael reached for Chelsea's hand, and she winced.

His gaze shot to her.

She held up the hand. "That scrape."

Michael turned to Draper. "Can you drop us at the doctor's house on the way back to town?"

"Sure."

They rode back to town in the backseat of the cruiser, and the young officer stopped at Dr.

Janecek's office. The doctor was finishing up with a patient, but his receptionist thought he could fit Chelsea in.

As they sat in the waiting area, Michael leaned toward Chelsea. "The fewer people who know what really happened, the better."

"What do you want me to say?"

"That we were out for a walk, and you slipped and hurt your hand."

"Okay."

A few minutes later, the receptionist called Chelsea's name. When she stood, Michael also got up and walked back with her.

The doctor looked surprised to see him, but he didn't make any comment as he gestured for Chelsea to sit down on the examination table. "What happened?"

"We were out for a walk, and I slipped."

Janecek inspected the hand. "This didn't just happen. It's starting to get infected."

"It was this morning. I thought it was okay at first."

"You didn't clean it properly," he said.

She glanced at Michael, then away. "I guess I was careless."

The doctor turned to him. "You should take better care of her, young man."

"Sorry," he said.

The doctor returned his attention to Chelsea. "I'm going to take a blood sample, just to make sure you haven't given yourself blood poisoning. Then I'll give you some antibiotics."

"Okay."

Michael looked at the diplomas on the wall. "You went to medical school in Prague?" he asked.

Janecek gave him a startled look. "Why, yes. I was born in the U.S., but I went back to my parents' country for medical school."

"How did you end up in Jenkins Cove?"

"The town needed a doctor, and I liked the pace of life here."

Deliberately, Janecek turned back to Chelsea.

Michael nodded, watching as the physician swabbed alcohol on Chelsea's arm and took the sample. Then he gave her an antibiotic shot and some pills for a follow-up. When they were finished, Michael excused himself to use the bathroom, then took a quick look around. Janecek seemed as if he was being evasive. Was he hiding something? Like maybe he'd faked his medical degree?

Or maybe he just wasn't used to anyone asking questions about his background. Still, it might be worth checking him out.

They were out of the office in less than half an hour.

"Was the doctor here when you were a little girl?" Michael asked.

"I think so. Why?"

"I'm just curious."

"I hope Aunt Sophie isn't worried," she said, changing the subject.

"Incredible as it may seem, we haven't been away all that long."

She nodded. "I guess it only seems like days since we started out this morning." She gave him a questioning look. "What happened to the gun?"

"I've still got it."

"Good. Because we might need protection."

"I'm glad you're taking this seriously."

"That's why I bought it in the first place."

"Yeah."

"Maybe we should call the state police and make sure they know about the grave site." She swallowed hard. "Thanks for not mentioning the ghost."

"I didn't think Draper or Hammer would deal with that too well."

When they stepped back into the House of the Seven Gables, Aunt Sophie gave them a questioning look. "What happened to the two of you? Chelsea, where's your coat?"

"It's a long story."

Her aunt's eyes narrowed. "I think you had better level with me. Something's been happening and you've been keeping me out of the loop, haven't you?"

"Yes," Chelsea admitted in a low voice.

"Come into the kitchen. I want both of you to tell me what's going on." She made a little sound.

"Well, not *everything*. There are some things I don't need to know."

Chelsea flushed, and Michael felt his face heat. Apparently Aunt Sophie didn't miss much.

In the kitchen they told her about the shooting incident and their escape.

"This is getting serious," Sophie murmured.

"I'm afraid so."

"It's lucky we're not having a lot of guests this week."

"Is that unusual?" Michael asked.

"Well, we wanted to relax after the party," Sophie allowed.

They talked for a while longer, and then Chelsea excused herself to call the garage.

After he'd showered and put his own clothes back on, he went up to her room. When he knocked, she called out, "Come in."

She was standing in the middle of the room, with wet hair and wearing one of the B & B's robes. She looked so sweet and vulnerable that his heart turned over.

"How are you?" he asked, crossing the room and taking her in his arms.

"Fine."

"You can't be, after what you've been through."

"I'm fine when you're holding me." She tipped her head up, and he brought his lips to hers for a kiss that quickly turned greedy.

"So, what are we going to do?" she asked when the kiss broke. "Do I sneak down to your room tonight, or do you sneak up here?"

"Do you think either one of those is a good idea?" he asked.

"You're right. It will be harder to explain your being up here. I'll come down to your room."

"Chelsea!"

"You don't want me?"

"Of course I want you."

She grinned and pulled the edge of the robe open a little, then guided his hand inside.

He made a low sound when he encountered her naked breast, and felt her nipple tighten under his touch.

"We can't do this now," he muttered, hearing his voice turn rough.

"I just want you to know what you'll be missing if you lock your door. It won't do you any good, anyway. I've got the key."

"Yeah. So I might as well surrender."

"Good decision."

He knew that if he didn't take his hand away, they were headed for the nearby bed. He pulled back and asked, "Can you do me a favor?"

"What?"

"Get Phil Cardon in here to do some work. I'd like to have a look in his tool kit. And his car. We might even find out something from the way he acts."

She thought for a moment. "There are several repairs we need done, and some painting. With the house almost empty, doing the work now would make sense."

"Do you mind having him do those things? I could pay for it, if that's a problem."

"No. We need to have the work done anyway. I'll call him after I get dressed."

Before Michael could get into trouble, he left the room.

CHELSEA DRESSED and walked downstairs to the office, where she called Phil.

"I was hoping you could do some repair work for us," she said. Quickly she outlined the projects. "When could you come?" she asked.

"I had a cancellation for tomorrow," he said.

"Perfect."

"Around nine?"

"Yes."

After transacting the business, she hung up, then stood looking out the window, suddenly overcome by everything that had happened since last night.

It had been quite a lot—starting with the ghost and ending with almost getting arrested. In between, she and Michael had made love. And she was getting ready to do it again tonight.

Things were moving very quickly with Michael. More quickly than they ever had in her life.

Well, she'd worry about that later, she told herself as she climbed the stairs to her room. Right now she was dead tired.

She lay down, intending to relax for a few minutes. Instead, she was instantly asleep.

MICHAEL EXPECTED TO SEE Chelsea that evening. But when he heard a knock at his door, he opened it and found Aunt Sophie standing there.

"In case you were planning on meeting Chelsea later, I thought I'd better warn you that she's sleeping. And she looks like she's down for the count."

He tried to keep his voice cool. "I appreciate your telling me."

"Things have changed between you," Aunt Sophie said.

He shifted his weight from one foot to the other but didn't answer.

Sophie gave him a long look, but mercifully, she said nothing else before turning on her heel and leaving.

In truth, Michael was also zonked by the day's ordeal. He went to bed early and woke up to the sound of pounding somewhere in the house.

Quickly he got up and dressed, then went into the dining room, where he found Chelsea waiting for him.

"Sorry," she murmured.

"About what?"

She lowered her voice. "Not coming to your room."

He stepped closer and cupped his hand over her shoulder. "We both needed to sleep."

"Still…"

He looked toward the kitchen and leaned forward so he could give her a quick kiss.

She stepped closer, leaning into him. They stood close together for several moments, and he drank in her familiar scent.

A noise in the kitchen made them both jump and move a few feet apart.

"Is that Phil working?" he asked.

"Yes."

"Keep him in the kitchen. I'm going to go out and look at his truck. If it looks like he's coming out, warn me."

She nodded and disappeared into the kitchen.

Quickly he exited through the front door and walked around to where the handyman had left his truck—the same one they'd seen him in the day before.

The door was unlocked, and Michael leaned inside. He found what he was looking for in the glove compartment—a handgun.

Before he could check to see if it had been fired, a sharp rap on the window made him slam the compartment closed and leap out of the truck.

He'd barely closed the door when Phil appeared.

The handyman gave him a long look. "Something I can do for you?"

"No. I was just catching a little air."

"Without your coat?"

"Yeah," he said, his eyes fixed on the man. "Like you."

"I'm only out here to get my paintbrushes and tray."

"I'm only out here for a few minutes," Michael countered.

Phil brushed past him and headed toward the tool locker in the truck bed.

Michael ducked back into the house, where Chelsea was waiting for him. "Thanks for the warning."

"I wonder if he thinks we're up to something."

"Don't know."

"You have a lot of experience with this cloak-and-dagger stuff?" she asked.

He shrugged. "A little."

"Where did you pick it up?"

He shrugged again. "Here and there."

He could have told her that it was a skill an investigative reporter needed, but he ducked the question by asking, "What's for breakfast?"

"French toast."

"Sounds wonderful."

In the dining room, he picked up a copy of the *Washington Post,* folded it to the editorial section and read some of the commentaries as he waited for his breakfast.

Phil exited the kitchen and walked through the

dining room, carrying his painting equipment. He gave Michael a sharp look as he passed.

Michael just kept reading the newspaper.

Aunt Sophie delivered his breakfast, and he began to eat. He was still sitting at the table when he heard voices in the kitchen.

Was that Phil talking to Aunt Sophie?

No, Phil had gone to some other part of the house. He could have come back in, though, through the kitchen door.

And he could be up to no good.

Quietly, Michael stood up and walked to the door. When he pushed it open a crack, he saw a man he didn't immediately recognize. Then he remembered the guy's name. Edwin Leonard.

He and Aunt Sophie were talking earnestly, both with their backs to him.

Taking the opportunity to find out what they were concerned about, he stayed where he was, eavesdropping.

"I don't like to be disloyal to Mr. Brandon," Leonard was saying as he hunched his shoulders and leaned closer to Sophie.

"Just because he's hiding papers, that's no reason to get upset," Aunt Sophie said gently.

"But I've been with him for years, and it's not like him to be so secretive."

"Well, if you're worried, you should go to the police," Aunt Sophie murmured.

"I've never trusted the cops," Leonard answered.

"Yes, well, I can understand why you don't think much of Chief Hammer."

"There's something about that man that sets my teeth on edge," Edwin muttered.

"I agree entirely."

A noise from behind him made Michael go rigid. Quietly he closed the door and turned—to find Chelsea staring at him.

"Can I help you?" she said, an edge in her voice.

Chapter Fifteen

Michael took several steps away from the door and turned to face her. "Edwin Leonard is upset about something. Something to do with Brandon Drake."

"It makes me uncomfortable when you listen in on Aunt Sophie."

"Well, it was actually Edwin. Maybe we've been looking in the wrong direction."

"Maybe," she conceded.

"It's got to do with Brandon Drake hiding some papers. Maybe you can find out more about it."

"If I can find a graceful way to do it."

Michael could see that Chelsea was on edge. He didn't blame her. He was on edge, too. He was just handling it differently.

He cleared his throat. "What's the name of that detective who was here from the state police?"

"Rand McClellan."

"I think I'm going to tell him what's been happening to us."

She answered with a tight nod.

"You don't approve?"

"I do. But I'm starting to wonder about my judgment."

He gave her a long look. He wanted to ask exactly what she meant. But he didn't want to push her into saying something he didn't want to hear.

"I wonder if Chief Hammer will think we're pulling rank on him," she whispered.

"The heck with Hammer. I want to make sure nothing happens to you."

He wanted to reach for her and hold on to her—to reassure himself that everything was okay between them. But the look in her eyes made him back away.

In his room he debated whether to call the barracks or just show up. He liked the idea of taking the detective by surprise, but he could be wasting a trip out there if the guy wasn't available. So he called.

Rand McClellan wasn't at his desk when Michael arrived at the barracks. He was outside on a basketball court behind the building, wearing sweatpants and a sweat jacket and dribbling a ball.

"Kind of informal, aren't we?" Michael asked as the detective passed the ball to him. He dribbled it a couple of times, then aimed for the basket, made the shot and passed the ball back.

Was this guy putting him on?

The cop dribbled the ball a few times and took a shot.

"You must have played in college," Michael commented.

"High school—like you."

Michael watched the ball hit the rim and circle before dropping into the basket. "You had to do some digging to find about my high school basketball days."

"But your article about the clients at that investment firm was pretty easy to find. Did ghosts bring you to Jenkins Cove?"

To hide his surprise, Michael bounced the ball, then shot again—and missed. "Okay, yeah."

"So, what do you want to know—if I think Chelsea Caldwell really did see a ghost?"

"No, I've changed my mind about the supernatural."

"Oh yeah? What happened?"

"Some weird stuff that you probably wouldn't believe."

"Try me."

"Let's just keep this on the factual level. I want to tell you that Chelsea's in danger." As he gave an account of the incidents of the past few days, the cop stopped dribbling and studied him. "Hammer share any of that with you?" Michael asked.

"Actually, no."

"Why do you think that is?"

McClellan shrugged. "It could be because I'm invading his territory."

"You think he doesn't want to find out who killed that girl?"

"Maybe."

"But you're not sure about his motives," Michael pressed.

"I try not to jump to conclusions."

"That's refreshing."

"I appreciate your stopping by," McClellan said. "And if you can keep me in the loop, I appreciate that, too." He handed Michael a card with a phone number. "That's my direct line."

"You have any leads on the case?" he asked McClellan. "Did you identify the woman who was murdered?"

"Nobody reported missing." The cop gave him a direct look. "It might be safer for you if you got out of town."

"Funny, that was the advice Hammer gave Chelsea. But she's not going anywhere, and neither am I. That would leave her unprotected."

"You aim to protect her?"

"I do." His gaze bored into the detective. "Have you taken her off your suspect list?"

"What makes you think she's on it?"

"She found the body."

McClellan sighed. "That's the only connection I can find."

"Good."

The detective turned toward the station, then spun back. He gave Michael a long, hard look. "A piece of advice, Mr. Bryant. Watch your back."

As Chelsea entered the office she remembered the unsettling feeling from earlier that day when she'd stepped into the kitchen. Edwin and her aunt had been talking but had gone quiet as soon as she stepped in.

Had they been talking about Brandon Drake? Or had the conversation turned personal?

She hadn't found out because almost as soon as she'd entered the room, Edwin excused himself, saying he needed to get back to Drake House.

Aunt Sophie had offered no insight when Chelsea had questioned her.

"The conversation was nothing you have to worry about," she'd said.

Since then, Chelsea had other things on her mind. Serious things. Like Michael. She'd rushed into an intimate relationship with a man she hardly knew, and now she was wondering if she'd moved too fast.

Michael kept surprising her with his expertise in what she'd called cloak-and-dagger skills. And when she'd asked him about it, he'd been evasive.

He reminded her more of a private investigator than a writer. Was he here in Jenkins Cove on some covert assignment he couldn't talk about?

An unsettling memory rattled her, and she went still. She remembered a handsome, smooth-talking art dealer she'd dated a year ago. Carl Whitman. He'd claimed he was interested in a relationship but she'd found out that what he really wanted was to get her paintings for a good price.

She winced. Was Michael doing something similar? Well, not with her work. With something else.

She clenched her hands into fists. Perhaps she was getting cold feet and was looking for reasons to put some distance between them.

Well, maybe she should do what she should have done in the first place—see what she could find out about him.

Pulling the chair up to the desk, she switched on the computer and opened a connection to the Internet.

Then she went to Google and typed in *Michael Bryant*. It was a common name, but since he was a writer, she could sort out which one he was.

Only, the citations weren't what she'd expected.

He'd written several books—one on the civil war in Rwanda, another on New Jersey mobsters and another on the rapid changes in technology.

And he had a whole slew of articles in prestigious national magazines.

She'd thought he was working on a novel. But all of his books were nonfiction.

So he'd come down here and misrepresented himself. At least, he'd let her and Aunt Sophie come to the wrong conclusions about him.

As she scanned more notations about his career, she quickly gathered that the topics he picked were generally something he wanted to debunk or expose.

So what did that mean for Jenkins Cove? What was he really doing down here?

With a tight feeling in her chest, she began searching for more evidence.

One of his recent articles had been about a Chicago investment broker whose clients were getting bilked by a medium. Michael had exposed the woman as a fraud.

The summary of the article set her teeth on edge. He'd certainly gone after the medium with a vengeance.

As Chelsea looked for more references, she found several instances where he'd participated in chat rooms or done guest blogs. One of the blogs was by a man who was writing snide comments about the current interest in psychic phenomena.

"I have to agree with you," Michael had written. "There's no scientific basis for belief in ghosts. People who claim to have seen them are obviously making a bid for attention. Take the case of a woman in Jenkins Cove, Maryland, who claimed to have seen a ghost when she was a little girl. Recently, she's come up with another story that can't be verified by any known facts."

Chelsea's heart started to pound as she stared at the entry. It was written the week before he'd come down here.

Michael was talking about her.

He hadn't come here to write something unfavorable about Jenkins Cove.

He had come here to write something unfavorable about *Chelsea Caldwell!*

No wonder he'd been abashed when she'd asked where he got his ideas. It was from his own nasty prejudices.

Just as she finished scrolling through the snide comments he'd written on the blog, the door to the office opened, and the man himself stepped in.

"Oh, there you are," he said. "I thought we could…"

She wanted to run and hide from this poseur who thought so little of her. Instead, she pushed back the chair and stood up, facing him squarely.

MICHAEL FELT his blood run cold as he looked wildly around the room. Unable to identify the problem, he rushed toward Chelsea.

"What is it? What's happened?" he asked as he stepped in front of her and grasped her shoulders.

He felt her go rigid. "Take your hands off me," she said in a voice he hardly recognized.

"What's wrong?" Even as he asked the question, he had a horrible suspicion of what she was going to say.

She stepped aside and pointed to the computer screen.

"Did you write this?" she asked in a voice as cold as ice.

He looked at the reply he'd made to the blog

entry and repressed a groan. Detective Rand McClellan wasn't the only one who had looked him up. Apparently Chelsea had decided to do it, too.

"That was before I knew you," he said.

"Yes, well, you should have kept it that way."

"That was my stupid uninformed opinion."

"You came to Jenkins Cove to write about me. To prove that I'd made up ghost stories to get attention—or maybe something worse."

He felt as if the floor had dropped out from under his feet. Still, he kept talking. "I can't deny that. But you know that's not what I think anymore."

She didn't seem to be listening. Either that or she didn't care what he had to say. "You've been using me," she spat out.

"No!"

"What would you call it?"

"I've fallen in love with you."

She answered with a mirthless laugh. "Oh, please. You saw an opportunity to get into my pants and you took it."

He could have argued that he'd kept himself from making love to her as long as humanly possible—given how much he wanted her. He could have told her that cold fear had gathered in his gut when he'd thought about her finding out his original motivation.

"Why did you pick on me?" she asked in a strangely quiet voice.

"A friend got me interested in the subject. He's an investment broker, and he found out a number of his clients were consulting a medium and losing money every time they followed her hot tips. Some of them got bilked out of their life savings. It made me remember something I'd repressed from my own childhood, when my mom consulted a medium after my father died. The woman got a lot of money out of her before she decided she wasn't really communicating with my dead father. I knew the woman was lying to her, and I had to stand there and watch it happen, because I was a kid and she wouldn't listen to me. I can't stand liars. And I thought you were one. That article in the *Gazette* said you'd been talking about ghosts."

"That was a damn lie. I never talked about it. The story got around, and the reporter assumed I had said something."

"Yes. As soon as I talked to you, I started doubting my assumptions."

"Yeah, right."

Ignoring the interjection, he plowed on. "And the better I got to know you, the more I realized you were absolutely honest. It only took a few days for me to realize you have a genuine gift."

"Thanks for the ringing endorsement. Now get out of here," she said. "I mean, pack up your things and get the hell out of my house."

"You can hate me," he said between clenched

teeth, "but I'm going to stay here to protect you until we find out who's trying to kill you."

"Did you make that up to get close to me?"

"Now you've really gone off the deep end," he muttered. "You think I made up someone shooting at us?"

"Maybe you were working with him. You insisted on taking the gun away from me. Then you never did shoot back at him."

"Because I couldn't see him! And then I would have announced that we were in that hole."

She snorted.

Seeing that nothing he said would make any difference at the moment, he turned and left the room.

"Pack your things and get out of here," she called after him. "I'll call Chief Hammer if you're not gone in an hour."

Ignoring her, he walked to his room and grabbed his jacket, then walked out of the house, where he stood breathing in the crisp December air. It made his chest hurt, although he suspected that simply breathing would be agony.

She'd ordered him out with vehemence and conviction. No way was he leaving, not when he'd lose his access to her. He had to change her mind about him. How, he wondered, when Chelsea wasn't going to give him a chance to get close to her again? And he wouldn't even blame her.

He should have confessed days ago. He'd tried to

do it yesterday but he'd only said half of what he needed to say to come clean.

Too bad he'd been a coward then.

As he stared across the harbor, he heard another door in the house open.

Quickly he charged around to the side yard in time to see Chelsea slam the door behind her and head toward the road—where the car had tried to run him over the first night in Jenkins Cove.

As he watched her stride away from the house, a car swerved around the corner. It stopped, and he saw someone inside roll down the window, although he couldn't tell who it was from where he was standing. Yet he sensed danger.

"Stay away from the car," he shouted. But either she was too far away to hear him, or she was too angry to pay attention to anything he said.

Briskly, she walked toward the vehicle and got in as Michael's warning died on the breeze. The car drove away.

Chapter Sixteen

Michael's heart leaped into his throat.

He had no proof that anything bad was happening—except for the telltale knot in his gut.

With only one goal in mind, he bolted toward the vehicle.

With a lurch, the car roared away. It was a silver Honda, one of the most common cars on the road.

His gaze dropped to the license plate, but it was obscured by mud. So he couldn't tell the cops what car to look for. And what would they do, anyway? He had no evidence of any crime.

He felt numb and cold as the car disappeared. He didn't have his car keys, and by the time he got them, the vehicle could be anywhere.

Frustration and agony bubbled over in a string of curses. He had no idea what he was going to do. Then an image leaped into his mind.

The psychomanteum. It was his only hope to find out who was in that car and why Chelsea had gotten inside.

The idea that he'd turn to the psychomanteum blew his mind. Yet he dashed into the house, then up to the third floor.

Inside the blackened room, he flipped on the light and looked around, seeing the chair, the black curtains and the mirror.

What should he do now?

He remembered the scene when he'd rushed in here and found Chelsea just after she'd been talking to Lavinia.

Lavinia. The ghost who had revealed the location of the graveyard. And the ghost who had shown them the hole in the ground where they could hide, and then illuminated it so they could see the tunnel. He hadn't seen the ghost but he'd seen that eerie glow.

He looked around and saw a box of matches on the table to the left of the door.

Quietly he walked around, lighting the candles; then he turned off the ceiling fixture. In the flickering light, he sat down and stared at his own reflection in the mirror.

Now came the hard part.

Tension tightened his chest. He would have felt like a fool doing this, except that he was desperate.

He sat there, staring at the mirror. But nothing seemed to happen. He shifted in his seat, feeling as if the walls of the room were closing in around him.

Finally, he spoke. "Lavinia, I need your help. Please, come to me."

Still, nothing happened, and Michael felt a lump of fear expand inside his chest.

CHELSEA STRUGGLED not to give away her terror. There were two men in the car—one driving and one holding a gun. The driver was the man she'd seen hanging around down by the dock. He wasn't anyone she knew. Not Ned Perry or Phil Cardon. But the gunman...

She knew *him*. It was Dr. Janecek. He'd been at the Christmas party. And yesterday he'd treated the wound on her hand. Now he was taking her away.

He'd called her over to the car before by saying he wanted to discuss her lab results. She hadn't even noticed the strange driver until she was in the backseat with a gun aimed at her head.

A few blocks from the House of the Seven Gables, the driver pulled into an empty garage and closed the door.

"Get out," the doctor ordered.

"What do you want with me?"

"Quiet," he snarled.

She got out of the car, trying and failing to keep from shaking.

"Hands behind your back."

She took her lower lip between her teeth as the driver pressed her hands behind her. Roughly, he wound duct tape around her wrists and then her ankles. When he came at her with another piece of tape for her mouth, she couldn't hold back a moan. For all the good it did her.

After they had finished, he carried her to another car and dumped her in the backseat like a sack of horse feed.

The door was open, and she could hear the men conferring a few yards away.

She didn't know the driver's name. But now she wished she'd paid more attention to him. He must also have been the man Michael had seen—the man who had escaped by boat.

"Listen, Franz, I'm tired of your acting on your own without waiting for my say-so," Janecek said.

"I was taking initiative."

"You're working for me, not the other way around. I need you to follow orders instead of making up jobs on your own. Go back and pick up Bryant so we can take care of both of them."

Chelsea tried to scream, "No." But the sound was muffled by the tape.

She'd been angry and hurt by Michael's betrayal when she ran out of the house. She was still angry. But now fear for him made her go cold all over.

And fear for herself. What were they planning to do with *her?*

The doctor got behind the wheel and pulled out of the garage.

Panic flooded through her system, making her feel as though her breath was choking off.

In the backseat, she tried to wrench her wrists apart, but it was no good. The tape was too tight and too firm. Terror threatened to sweep away all rational thought, but she struggled to rise above it, to make her mind function logically.

She remembered coming outside and how, just before she'd gotten into the car, she'd spotted Michael.

He'd seen her.

Either he'd seen that the doctor had a gun, or he'd sensed she was in danger, because he came running to save her. Only it was already too late.

Now he had no idea where to look for her.

From the front seat, the doctor spoke to her. "You couldn't leave well enough alone," he said, his voice regretful.

Her only thought was of Michael. He'd said he loved her, and like a fool she'd ignored him. Now she'd never get the chance to see him again.

BACK AT THE House of the Seven Gables, Michael struggled against his fear and frustration. Again, his pleas were met only by silence.

Unable to stay in the chair, he stood up and paced from one end of the psychomanteum to the other. When his agony bubbled over, he shouted, "You have to help me. Chelsea is in danger. I'll do anything it takes to save her."

"Will you?"

He hadn't really expected an answer, which was

why the voice in his ear was so startling. When he whirled around, he saw nothing. Or maybe he did. Maybe he detected a small wavering in the air.

"Lavinia?"

"Yes," the voice answered. He couldn't be sure if she'd spoken aloud or in his head. But he knew she had a thick accent. Russian or somewhere else in that part of the world.

"You have to help me," he gasped out.

"Why should I?"

FROM WHERE SHE LAY on the backseat, Chelsea could see the upper stories of buildings and the tops of trees passing by. When the view switched to only trees, she knew they were heading out of town. After what she judged was a few miles, they turned onto a bumpy road.

Branches pressed in on either side of the car, and she felt shocked when she recognized where they were headed.

This was the road to the old warehouse where she and Michael had gone a few days ago.

Silently, she called out to her only hope.

Michael, please, I need you. I'm at the old warehouse. The place where we went the other day. The place where you fell into that trap.

Please. Please come find me here.

She felt she was sending the message out into a

black hole, where it would never emerge into the sunlight again.

Michael wasn't going to find her here. She was on her own, and she had to save herself.

The car stopped abruptly.

Dr. Janecek got out and walked away from the car. Then she heard a scraping sound. Moments later he was back and driving into the warehouse through the open doors.

He got out again and she could see him walking around to the trunk. He got something out, something she couldn't see because it was below the level of the windows. Then he walked back to the trunk again. Finally, he opened the back door of the car, sat her up and hauled her out. Picking her up, he carried her a few yards away and laid her on a flat surface. A padded table.

Next he secured the lower half of her body to the table with straps. Then he cut the tape on her hands.

When she tried to lunge at him, he leveled a blow to her face. Stars flashed in front of her eyes.

Too stunned to move, she could only lie there as he secured her hands to straps at the side of the table. Then he cut the tape on her ankles and strapped her feet the way he had her hands.

When he stepped back, staring at her, the look on his face made her stomach churn.

"What…what are you going to do?" she asked.

"Solve two problems at once. Too bad you were

poking your nose in where it didn't belong. If you'd just driven by a little later, we would have had that woman buried. And you never would have gotten a chance to interfere."

"Please. Let me go," she begged.

He laughed, and it wasn't a pleasant sound. "So you can go straight to the cops? Of course not. But you're going to help me out. I have a buyer for a heart. And you're a match. I established that when I took that blood sample from you the other day."

MICHAEL STRUGGLED TO SPEAK around the constriction in his throat. He'd come to Jenkins Cove thinking that ghosts were total nonsense. Now here he was in the psychomanteum throwing himself on the mercy of a spirit.

From skeptic to true believer in a heartbeat.

In answer to the ghost's question, the truth came shooting out of his mouth with the force of a volcano breaking through the surface of the earth.

"You have to help me find Chelsea because I love her. And it's my fault she's in trouble. She went storming out of the house because she was mad at me. If anything happens to her, I'll never forgive myself."

Lavinia said nothing, and he felt his heart pounding as agonizing seconds ticked by.

When she spoke, it wasn't what he wanted so desperately to hear. "Why was she mad at you?"

He gulped. "Because before I came to Jenkins

Cove, I was mouthing off about how she must be a fraud."

"A fraud because she claimed she'd seen me?"

"Yes," he answered. "And now, if I have to get down on my knees and beg you to help me find her, I'll do it." He dragged in a breath and let it out. "I'll do it *now*."

He climbed out of the chair and sank to his knees beside it.

"Help me," he said again. "Please help me."

When he had finished pleading, he held his breath, waiting for an answer. And for long moments, he thought Lavinia was going to leave him in agony.

Then, to his profound relief, her voice whispered next to his ear, "Dr. Janecek is holding her at the old warehouse."

The words were so unexpected that he blinked. Was she putting him on? "Dr. Janecek? Why would he do that?"

Her ghostly voice turned flinty. "He's been bringing people into Jenkins Cove for years. Illegal aliens. From Eastern Europe. He speaks those languages, so he can communicate with them."

Michael's brain was on overload. They'd been to see the doctor after Chelsea hurt her hand. If Janecek was behind the killings, then they'd played right into his hands.

"What…what does he bring them in for?" he managed to ask in a cracked voice.

"Some are sex slaves. Some paid a lot of money to get into the country. Or they might pay for their passage with a kidney. Like me. Only I didn't plan to do that. I saved my money so I could pay up front, but then the doctor said I had to donate a kidney anyway."

The ghost was silent for several moments; then she made a strangled sound.

"What?"

"You must hurry. Chelsea is in grave danger. The doctor is going to take her heart for a transplant patient."

Michael scrambled to his feet. When he almost lost his balance, he grabbed the back of the chair to steady himself. "Her heart," he gasped. "Oh God, not her heart."

He dashed out of the room and pounded down the steps to the ground floor. First he ran to the living room and picked up the phone. Fumbling in his pocket, he pulled out the paper where he'd written down Rand McClellan's number.

Centuries passed while the phone rang at the other end of the line. When McClellan answered, Michael started to shout at him. Then he realized it was a recorded message. The detective wasn't there.

All Michael could do was spit out his message and pray the guy got it. "Chelsea is being held at the old warehouse on the edge of town where I told you I fell into that hole. Janecek is going to kill her."

Slamming down the receiver, he charged out of the room and onto the porch.

Then he thought maybe he should tell Sophie to alert Chief Hammer. He'd just called out to her when a voice spoke behind him.

"Hold it right there."

He whirled around again. Instead of Aunt Sophie, he saw a man step out of the bushes beside the house and onto the oyster-shell path. He was of medium height and weight. There was nothing much distinctive about him except that he was holding an automatic pistol.

"Hands up."

Michael stared at him. "Who the hell are you?" But even as the question tumbled out of him, he was pretty sure he knew the answer. It was the man who had been watching the house. The man who had tried to run him over. The man who had tried to kill Chelsea in the kitchen with the blender and the water on the floor, before escaping in a boat from the dock. And probably the man who had hunted them out in the bog.

"It don't matter who I am. You're coming with me."

"Where?"

"You'll find out soon enough."

THE DOCTOR TURNED AWAY from Chelsea, and she saw him set up another table a few feet from where she lay. When he had it in place, he walked back to the car and retrieved a black bag he'd brought. His back to her, he laid out a white towel, then began taking out shiny, frightening instruments.

Once more he returned to the car trunk, and this time he took out a carrying case. She recognized it from television programs she'd seen. It was the kind of container they used to transport human organs.

She wanted to scream, "No. Let me go. I haven't done anything to hurt you."

But she knew that was a lie. She'd done something to hurt him the moment she'd driven to the police station. She'd gotten in the way of his illegal operation, and he wasn't going to allow her to trip him up that way.

She pulled at the straps that secured her to the table, but she was held firmly in place. She wasn't going anywhere. This was it.

In a few moments she would be dead. Did the doctor plan to give her anesthetic when he cut her open? The question was too horrible to contemplate.

She squeezed her eyes shut for a moment because that was the only way she could be alone. She'd been a fool. She understood that now. But it was too late. All her hopes and dreams would end right here, in this warehouse.

She'd rushed out of the house because she'd been so hurt when she'd read Michael's comments on that blog. But she knew he had changed his mind since coming to Jenkins Cove. She knew he'd tried to tell her about it before he'd made love to her. But he'd lost his nerve, and she understood why. He'd known she'd be angry and hurt. He'd told her part of it and he'd probably been hoping to find the right time to tell her the rest. Only she'd gotten ahead of him and found it out herself.

Oh Lord. If she'd only let him explain, she wouldn't be in this mess now.

But his words on that blog had felt like the worst kind of betrayal—because she'd fallen in love with him.

Now she was in this old warehouse, strapped to a table, about to die. And she wouldn't get a chance to tell Michael what she felt for him.

"Michael, I forgive you," she whispered in a voice too low for the doctor to hear. "I wish I could tell you that. I wish I could tell you I love you."

A whisper of sound answered her. Not Michael. Someone else.

Chelsea looked around her. The air seemed to stir. "Lavinia?"

The ghost didn't answer, but Dr. Janecek spun around, his eyes fixed on her. "What did you say?"

"Lavinia," she said in as strong a voice as she could muster. "She's here."

"She can't be. She's dead."

"But she came back. She spoke to me in the psychomanteum."

"That's just a bunch of hooey."

"Is it? Then how do I know her name?"

"You found the list of people coming in that shipment," he shot back.

"Shipment! That's a wonderful way to put it. And where do you think I would have seen it?"

"You came to my office. That Michael Bryant guy wasn't with you every moment. He must have gone snooping around."

"Is that where you keep your lists?"

"You know I do!"

She struggled to hold her voice steady, to sound logical. "You're clutching at straws."

The doctor's eyes narrowed. "Don't try to turn this around. You're the one in trouble. You've been snooping into my business, and now you're just trying to stall me, to keep yourself alive for a few more minutes."

"Go on thinking that," Chelsea said in a firm voice. "Until the cops come to get you."

"I know you didn't call the cops," he shot back.

Ignoring the comment, Chelsea said, "That wasn't you the other day out in the marsh shooting at us."

"Hardly. I don't go in for tramping around in the mud unless I have to. That was my assistant, Franz Kreeger—the man who was with me in the car. But you're not going to get a chance to tell that to anyone."

"He killed Lavinia?"

When Janecek didn't answer, she asked another

question. "Why are you doing this? I mean all of it—not just the part about me."

"For money."

"You don't need it!"

He turned to glare at her. "How would you know what I need? I grew up in a family where there was never enough of anything to go around. I decided I wasn't going to live that way ever again."

"So you took advantage of helpless people?"

"Stop asking questions," he said with a snarl in his voice.

Instead, she changed the subject again. "I understand why you went after me. But why did Franz Kreeger try to run over Michael when he first arrived in town?"

"Did he?"

"You know he did."

"We were keeping tabs on you and everybody who came to the House of the Seven Gables, in case they were there to help you make trouble for us. We knew that Michael Bryant was a journalist. But I didn't tell Franz to run him down. If he tried it, that was his idea."

So the doctor had been smart enough to look Michael up, long before she'd thought of it. Score one for him.

More than one. Because she was the person strapped to the table and he was the one with the surgical instruments.

As her thoughts whirled, the air behind the doctor shivered, then changed and thickened. Chelsea felt a sudden surge of hope. She saw a figure standing behind the doctor. A woman she could see right through.

"Lavinia?" she called out again as something unseen rushed at Janecek. He must have felt it, because his face took on a look of horror as the phantom flew past him.

Chapter Seventeen

Michael stood facing the man with the gun, his mind churning as it sought a way out.

Then from the corner of his eye, he saw someone else. Aunt Sophie. She had come around the side of the house and gotten behind the man. In her hands she held a pot of something steaming.

He could guess her plan. But he could see that she was putting herself in terrible danger.

He wanted to shout at Sophie to get out of there. Duck for cover. Call the cops. But trying to communicate with her now was out of the question. The best he could do was keep the gunman's attention focused squarely on him so that Sophie wouldn't get hurt.

He cleared his throat and raised his head slightly. "Put down the gun."

The man laughed. "You must be kidding. You're coming with me."

"And if I don't?"

"I shoot you right here."

Michael tipped his head to one side. "Don't you think that will attract a lot of attention?"

"Not before I get the hell out of here."

"This time you didn't bring a boat, did you? You'll have to leave by car. That'll be more dangerous for you."

Behind the man, Aunt Sophie raised the pot and hurled the steaming contents at the gunman's neck.

The man screamed as hot liquid hit him, and the smell of cinnamon filled the air.

The gun fired. But Michael was already out of the way.

The man dropped the weapon and began scrabbling at his burning skin, but the hot liquid seared him like napalm.

Michael kicked the pistol aside, then leaped at the gunman, throwing him to the ground, pummeling him with his fists.

"You bastard," he shouted. "Chelsea better be all right, or I'll kill you."

"Michael, no," Aunt Sophie shouted. "Get away from him. I have him covered."

He looked up to see that Chelsea's aunt had grabbed the gun and was holding it in a two-handed grip like a lady detective in a cop show. Apparently Chelsea wasn't the only woman in the family who knew how to handle a firearm.

As he stepped away from the man on the ground,

a noise filtered into his consciousness. It was a police siren heading this way.

"I called the cops before I came out," Aunt Sophie said.

Two squad cars screeched to a halt in the parking area beside the house. Chief Hammer leaped out of one. The deputy named Sam Draper leaped out of the other.

"What's going on?" the chief demanded.

"This man tried to kill Michael Bryant," Sophie said, the gun never wavering from the suspect. "I was making Christmas candles, and I threw hot wax on him."

"He's working with Dr. Janecek," Michael added. "The doctor has Chelsea out at the old warehouse. He's going to kill her. We've got to get out there."

"That's a lie," the guy on the ground shouted. "These people attacked me. The old lady pulled a gun."

Michael answered with a curse. If they all ended up at the police station sorting through truth and lies, it would be too late for Chelsea.

Lord, what was he going to do, steal a police cruiser and go roaring out of town?

The tactic had a certain amount of appeal. The trouble was, there were two cop cars here. The officers would chase him, maybe shoot at him. And if he ended up wrecking the car, he was no closer to helping Chelsea than he was standing here.

FROM HER POSITION on the table, Chelsea watched the doctor turn back to his instruments. He sorted through the tools he'd laid out, then picked up a scalpel and examined it.

Apparently satisfied, he advanced on Chelsea. As she saw light gleaming off the blade, she tried to squirm away, but the straps held her fast.

The doctor had taken two steps forward when something whooshed at him again. This time it wasn't just one phantom. The air in the warehouse shimmered with shapes Chelsea could barely see. Suddenly the shapes took form. The room seemed to be filled with a whole host of people. Men, women and children crowded into this one enclosure. She knew they had come to help her. These must be the victims Dr. Janecek had killed. Yet he didn't seem to know they were there.

Or did he?

A low buzz filled the air, like the buzzing of a thousand bees. The doctor raised his head, looking around, his gaze darting from one corner of the warehouse to the other.

THOUGH MICHAEL WANTED TO SHOUT at Hammer or, better yet, rush the cop, he spoke slowly and clearly. "Let's try again. Dr. Janecek is holding Chelsea out at the abandoned warehouse southwest of town. The one at the site of the old dock on Jenkins Creek. He's been using it to bring in illegal aliens. This guy was helping him. He's the man who murdered that woman out along the road. He's the one who shot at us out in the marsh. He and Janecek have been stalking Chelsea ever since she saw the murder. If you keep standing here, questioning me, Chelsea is going to end up dead and you are going to be responsible. Do you want that on your conscience?"

The chief looked uncertain.

Aunt Sophie stood with her hands on her hips. When she spoke, her voice had taken on a hard edge. "Charlie Hammer, you know me. Would I throw a pot of hot wax on an innocent man?"

The chief looked from her to the man on the ground.

"Well, consider this," she continued, her face as stern as a teacher who has caught one of her students carving her initials on his desk, "if you let my niece die, I will never forgive you. And I will make sure the whole town knows what happened. Jenkins Cove is a small place. Is that how you want to be remembered?"

Without answering her, Hammer turned to his deputy. "Take the guy to the station."

"I'll sue you," the man shouted as Draper escorted him to one of the cruisers and ducked his head as he pushed him inside.

"I doubt it," Hammer muttered, then turned to Michael. "How do you know Chelsea is at the warehouse?"

Michael's throat clogged. What would happen if he told Hammer the truth?

Once again, Aunt Sophie came to the rescue. Gesturing toward the other police cruiser, she said, "That man you're taking away told us."

The audacity of the lie made Michael blink. Neither one of them had heard the guy say anything of the kind. He had to believe, then, that Aunt Sophie had known he was in the psychomanteum and knew where he'd gotten the information.

His gaze shot to her, and she answered with a tiny nod.

In the middle of the silent exchange, Hammer spoke. "Okay, but was he telling the truth?"

"It's our only lead," Michael argued. "And if we don't get there in time, we'll all be sorry."

To Michael's profound relief, Hammer nodded. "Let's go."

Michael climbed into the police car with the chief, and they sped off.

"You know the turnoff to that old warehouse down by the water? The place where I fell into a trap."

"I know where you mean."

Siren blaring, they raced through town, and sped up when they reached the highway. Still, Michael's heart was in his throat. If he was going to get to Chelsea in time, every second counted.

He had another worry, as well, one that twisted

his gut. He couldn't be perfectly sure that the police chief and the doctor weren't working together.

THE DOCTOR ADVANCED on Chelsea, still clutching the scalpel in his hand. He raised his arm, and she wanted to close her eyes as the arm came down in a slashing motion. But, to her astonishment, instead of slicing into her chest, the blade slashed through the strap that held her right hand to the side of the table.

"What the hell?" he cried out as he saw what he had done. Obviously it hadn't been what he'd intended, but somehow the mass of ghosts in the room had influenced his actions.

She saw his features firm, and she knew that he was fighting their power over him.

"No!" he shouted as he raised the instrument again, but this time Chelsea wasn't helplessly strapped down. She was able to crash the fist of her free hand into his mouth. Howling in pain, he toppled backward, landing against the table of instruments and scattering them across the floor.

While he was trying to sort himself out, Chelsea rolled to the side, so that she could reach the other strap. Desperately she fumbled with the leather.

Janecek was on his feet, advancing toward her again.

Teeth gritted, she pulled at the buckle on the strap, trying to loosen her other hand. But her fingers were clumsy, and she couldn't pull the end of the leather through the buckle.

"You won't get away," he swore. "Even if I can't get your heart, you won't get out of here alive."

The doctor had almost reached her when the air around him seemed to thicken again. In a surge of translucent shapes, the ghosts were coming after him, trying to keep him from getting to her.

But she saw the determination in his eyes. He was going to finish her off so she couldn't talk—then get the hell out of here.

As she was still fastened down by one hand and her two feet, the best she could do was roll away from the doctor, turning over the table and crashing to the floor.

For a moment she was stunned. Then Janecek leaped around the table, coming at her again. With a growl of anger, he slashed at her, the blade slicing through the fabric of her shirt and into her flesh.

She cried out in pain, but she wouldn't give up. One of her legs had come free of its strap in the fall, and she kicked out at him, landing a blow to his gut.

He howled again, then dived for her.

Before he could inflict another slash into her flesh, she saw something in back of him. This time it was not a ghost. It was a man—running at full speed across the floor.

It was Michael.

She screamed his name. "Watch out. He's got a scalpel."

As Michael closed in on the doctor, Janecek whirled around and swung his arm. Michael ducked under the knife, landing a blow on the man's chin.

Behind Michael, another figure entered the warehouse. Chief Hammer.

He ran forward, his service weapon in his hand.

"Stop or I'll shoot," he shouted.

Both Michael and the doctor ignored him. With the men struggling, there was no way Hammer could get a clear shot at the doctor—if that was his intended target. She couldn't be absolutely sure which man he wanted to shoot.

Michael grabbed the arm with the scalpel, bending it back so that the doctor screamed in pain.

"Drop it," Michael shouted, "or I'll break your damn arm."

The doctor screamed again as the pressure increased. Finally he dropped the blade and lay breathing hard.

"Cuff him," Michael panted.

As he heard the words, the doctor made a desperate lunge for safety. Michael tackled him again and held him in place. "Do it now!"

For a heartbeat the chief hesitated. Then he rushed forward and slapped handcuffs on the doctor. Michael ran to Chelsea. When he saw that she was cut, he gasped. "You're bleeding."

"It's not bad."

"It better not be."

He knelt beside her, freeing her other hand and her leg, then pulling a strip of cloth from the table and pressing it to her wounded shoulder.

Chief Hammer was starting back toward them when something happened, something that made her eyes bug out.

From out of nowhere came a shriek that sounded like the protest—or the triumph—of a long-dead spirit finally evening the score with the living.

Then others took up the cry, and the air around them was filled with what sounded like a thousand unseen voices.

"What the hell is that?" Chief Hammer cried out, running toward Michael and Chelsea. He crouched beside her as something flew over their heads. Something they could barely see.

"Keep your head down," Michael called as he bent over Chelsea, gathering her close, sheltering her body against the overturned table.

The air inside the warehouse churned and boiled. Darts of light sailed over and around them as the sound rose, like some kind of indoor windstorm. And above the wailing of the wind, they heard Janecek screaming.

Chapter Eighteen

Suddenly, it all stopped. The wind, the churning of the air, the noise.

In the utter silence, Hammer asked, "What was that?"

"Ghosts," Michael said. He wasn't looking at the chief. He was looking at Chelsea.

"What do you mean, ghosts?" the chief snapped.

"Couldn't you feel them, hear them?" Michael asked, his gaze still on her.

"I don't know what all that was." Hammer stumbled to his feet and crossed the floor, where he knelt beside the handcuffed man.

"He's not breathing." Bending lower, he began administering artificial respiration.

"I think you're wasting your time," Michael muttered.

Another voice spoke from the door. Michael's head jerked up, and he saw Rand McClellan and a state patrolman standing in the doorway. "I got your message. It looks like I got here for the mop-up."

"Chelsea's hurt," Michael answered. "The doctor was going to take out her heart, but he only cut her shoulder."

McClellan winced. Reaching into his pocket, he pulled out his cell phone and called 911, reporting on Chelsea and the doctor.

While the detective was talking to the dispatcher, Michael stood and stripped the rest of the padding off the table, then lifted Chelsea and laid her on it, so that she was no longer sprawled on the cold floor. "How are you?"

"I'm fine now," Chelsea answered. "Thanks to you—and the ghosts." She kept her gaze on Michael as she spoke.

"Yeah, the ghosts," he answered.

"Where did they go?" she murmured.

"I think they went to their rest."

Chelsea nodded and closed her eyes. She was still feeling dazed and still unable to completely come to grips with everything that had happened. Now that the emergency was over, she struggled to hold herself together.

"I'm so sorry," Michael said in a gritty voice.

Her eyes blinked open again, and she shook her head. "No, I was stupid to run out of the house. You warned me to stay inside. But I was too angry to think."

"It's not your fault. I…hurt you."

The sound of a siren in the distance made him glance around.

Minutes later, paramedics rushed into the room. One headed for the doctor, the other ripped the top of her shirt and began examining her wound.

As he worked on her, she heard his partner call out. "The doctor's gone."

"What killed him?" Chief Hammer demanded.

"I can't determine that. You'll have to wait for the report from the medical examiner."

"You need your shoulder stitched," the medic told Chelsea.

"I want to talk to the chief first," she answered.

He heard her. Looking uncomfortable, he crossed back to her.

"Dr. Janecek told me he was bringing illegal aliens into the country," she said. "Some of the women were being sold into sexual slavery. Some of them had to pay for their passage with a kidney or other organ."

The chief winced.

Rand McClellan, who had been listening to the exchange, walked over and addressed the chief. "What do you know about that?"

"Nothing," Hammer answered, but the look in his eyes made her skeptical. Perhaps, she told herself, he was just too shell-shocked by his experience with the ghosts.

"He told me he was going to take my heart for a transplant," Chelsea told him.

The chief swore and strode out of the building.

"He knows more than he's saying," Michael muttered as the other medic bent over Chelsea.

She nodded.

So did McClellan. His mouth firmed. "I should have suspected the doctor. That woman whom you saw murdered—she'd had a kidney removed."

Chelsea gasped. "Why didn't you tell me?"

"That was information confidential to the investigation. I checked at a bunch of hospitals, and I couldn't find where the operation had been done. I should have started checking local doctors."

"That doesn't mean you would have found anything," Chelsea murmured. "He'd been getting away with it for years."

She stopped speaking as the EMTs wheeled in a stretcher.

"We'll take you to the hospital, Ms. Caldwell."

She looked at Michael. "Can he ride with me?"

"Yes."

McClellan and his patrol officer were conferring as the EMTs wheeled her past. Michael climbed into the ambulance beside her, but there was no chance to talk privately.

Then, when they arrived at the hospital, the doctor asked him to leave while he cleaned and stitched her cut.

"Draper's waiting to take your statement," Michael said when he came back into the room.

"What should I tell him?"

"The truth."

She gave Michael a long look. "About the ghosts attacking the doctor?"

Michael sighed. "Maybe you want to leave that part out."

"Why?" she pressed.

"Because it just makes people think you're a nut."

"But that's no longer your personal opinion?"

"You know it's not. Or if you're a nut, then I am, too. Because I went into the psychomanteum and begged Lavinia to tell me where to find you."

Her eyes widened. "You did?"

"Yeah. How do you think I figured out where you were?"

"I didn't know."

A knock on the door interrupted the conversation. It was Draper, who asked if she'd mind reporting what happened. She gave him an account of her kidnapping. Then she said, "And there's another guy who was working with the doctor."

"Franz Kreeger," Draper answered. "He tried to kill Mr. Bryant and your aunt."

Chelsea sucked in a sharp breath as her gaze shot to Michael. "I didn't know about that."

"We haven't had much time to talk."

Michael turned to the deputy. "So you believe us and not Kreeger?"

"There was evidence in his car linking him to the

doctor. We also found a woman's purse with blood-stains. We think it will match the blood of the woman you saw murdered," he said to Chelsea. "I've already talked to Detective McClellan. He'll be over in the morning to collect the evidence and take Kreeger into custody."

"Glad to hear it," Michael murmured.

The officer shifted his weight from one foot to the other, then cleared his throat. "There's something I want to say."

Both Michael and Chelsea instantly tensed.

"I want to apologize," Draper said. "That report you turned in about the murder... I told my wife about it and she told her friends. That's how the story about the ghost got around town. I'm hoping you'll forgive me."

"She had everybody whispering about me," Chelsea said.

Michael slung a protective arm over her shoulder.

"And now they're going to be talking about how you broke up a very nasty human smuggling operation and an organ transplant ring," Michael said.

"I'd rather they didn't."

"They won't get it from me," Draper vowed. "But it's news. It'll be in the *Gazette*."

"Yes," she answered.

The young officer cleared his throat. "Do you need me for anything else?"

Michael figured this was a good time to get some

concessions out of the guy. "Actually, we could use a ride back to the House of the Seven Gables." He turned toward Chelsea, who was wearing a hospital gown instead of her blood-soaked blouse. "And if there's a shirt and coat she could wear, we'd appreciate it."

"I think the nurses can lend her some scrubs," Draper said. "I'll see what I can round up."

When the guy had left, Chelsea sighed. "He caused me a lot of trouble, but he didn't mean to do it. That murder was big news in Jenkins Cove and a big deal for the local cops."

"You don't hold a grudge."

"I'd like to put it behind me."

He nodded, marveling that she could let it go. When a nurse brought back scrubs, Michael stepped out while the woman helped Chelsea dress.

Fifteen minutes later, they were met at the door of the B & B by an anxious Aunt Sophie.

"Oh, Chelsea," she exclaimed, eyeing the hospital outfit her niece was wearing. "Are you all right? I was so worried before the detective called."

Chelsea looked questioningly at Michael.

"McClellan called her from the warehouse. Then I gave her an update while you were getting stitched up," he answered.

"Come into the living room and sit down. I was so nervous after you left that I went into the kitchen and started baking. We have apricot nut bread, spice cookies and cinnamon buns."

Chelsea laughed, then sank onto the sofa. Michael stood awkwardly in the middle of the room. He was bursting to speak to her about the two of them. But it didn't look as though that was going to happen anytime soon.

"Sit next to me," Chelsea murmured.

Sophie bustled off, and Michael sat.

"We have to talk about us," he said, hearing the gritty sound of his own voice.

"As soon as we can get away. But right now you're going to tell me about what happened with that man—Franz Kreeger."

"He was holding a gun on me. I assume he was planning to take me out to the warehouse and finish me off, but your aunt threw a pot of hot wax at him."

Chelsea winced, just as Aunt Sophie came back into the room with a plate of goodies.

As she set them down, she said, "I knew there was something sinister going on in Jenkins Cove."

"You did?" Chelsea asked.

"Yes. But I couldn't prove it. Anyway, who'd listen to a nutty old woman?"

"You're not nutty," Chelsea said quickly.

"Of course I am. I have that psychomanteum upstairs. Don't think I don't know some people talk about me like I'm cracked. But I knew there were ghosts here and I knew that they could tell you—" She stopped and swallowed, then looked directly at Chelsea. "They could tell you what was wrong. That's why I asked you to come back and help me here."

Chelsea drew in a sharp breath. "You what?"

"But you weren't ready to deal with the ghosts," Sophie finished. She looked down at her hands. "It made sense when I thought of it. I didn't know I was going to put you in danger. I'm sorry."

"You didn't! It was seeing the ghost out on the road that started it."

Michael slid over and put his arm around her, drawing her close.

"No. It started with your seeing that other ghost— fifteen years ago," Sophie said. "I kept praying that you'd finish what you began."

Chelsea nodded. "I tried so hard to forget about that."

"And it came back to haunt you," her aunt said. "Let's stop talking about it now. Eat some of the cookies I made."

For the next twenty minutes, they ate cookies and drank mulled cider while they told Sophie about what had happened in the warehouse. Finally Sophie gave her niece a critical inspection. "You look done in. You should get some rest."

Michael scuffed his foot against the carpet, wondering if he was going to have to let Chelsea go up, then follow her when the coast was clear.

Sophie waved her hand. "Both of you might as well go on up to her bedroom. I can see you want to be alone with her, Michael. I just had some things I needed to get off my chest."

Grateful to escape, Michael helped Chelsea up the stairs. At the entrance to her room, he hesitated. But she pulled him inside, closed the door and wrapped her arms around him.

"I'm sorry," they both said at once.

"Let me get this off my chest," he begged. "I'm sorry I didn't tell you why I'd come to Jenkins Cove. And I'm sorry I didn't believe you from the beginning." He cleared his throat. "There's something else I should say. From the moment I got here, the ghosts tried to tell me I was wrong. When I left the house that first night, Lavinia or another one followed me down the street."

"She did?"

"Yeah. She gave me this really spooky feeling, but I didn't want to believe anything weird was happening so I convinced myself I was imagining things." He sighed. "Now what are you apologizing for?"

"For storming out of the house so Janecek could scoop me up."

"You didn't know he was out there."

"But you'd warned me to be careful. I should have paid attention to that. I could have gotten us both killed."

"If you hadn't gone out, Kreeger would probably have broken in and killed your aunt before going after us."

She winced.

When he pulled her close, she gasped.

"Your shoulder. I'm sorry."

"It's not that bad. Especially with the painkillers they gave me."

While he was holding her, he said what he'd been bursting to tell her since the warehouse. "I love you, Chelsea. I hope you can forgive me."

She tipped her head up so that she could meet his eyes. "I love you, too. That's why I was so upset."

He gathered her to him, lowering his head and covering her mouth with his. His kiss conveyed all the passion he'd kept bottled up inside as he'd waited to be alone with her. When the kiss broke, she began to speak.

"When I was strapped to that table in the warehouse, all I kept thinking of was how I wouldn't get a chance to tell you I love you."

"Thank God you did. Because of Lavinia."

"And you. Janecek was still trying his damnedest to kill me when you got there. He thought that if I was dead, he could still keep his secret. He didn't know the cops had already arrested Kreeger."

Michael held on to her, vowing he would never let her go. "So is it too soon to ask you to marry me?" he asked softly.

She raised her head and looked into his eyes. "It's pretty fast. But I don't need to think about the answer." She smiled. "It's yes."

"Oh, Chelsea, you've made me so happy." Then an inconvenient truth struck him.

"What is it?" she whispered. "You're having second thoughts?"

"No. I'm thinking about supporting a wife. I mean, I'm going to have to give up the current book, which means I have to scrounge around for another topic, and it may be a few months before I get anything started."

She kept her gaze fixed on him. "You can do the same book. Well, partly the same book."

"How?"

"Why don't you make it an investigation of which supernatural claims are real? You can start with the Jenkins Cove ghosts."

"That's a fantastic idea. But would you really want me to write about what happened here?"

"Wouldn't that give the book more authenticity?"

"Yes. But I don't want to do anything that would upset you."

She grinned. "I'm the one who suggested it, remember?" Before he could raise any more objections, she brought his mouth back to hers for a long, drugging kiss.

When he finally raised his head, he looked down at her and smiled.

She looked a bit unsure.

"What is it?"

"I know Aunt Sophie said she asked me back to

Jenkins Cove to contact the ghosts, but she really does need help. Is it going to be a problem living here? I mean, no matter how you spin it, my aunt is a little nutty."

"I'm adjusting. To the psychomanteum—and the cookies. Besides, this would be a perfect place to write. Maybe I can even start that novel I told you about." He grinned. "Which gives me another idea. If I sell my house in D.C., where the prices are sky-high, we'll be rolling in cash."

"Hold off on that until you're sure."

"I'm sure. The luckiest day of my life was the day I called to get a room here."

"Lucky for both of us. We just had to work our way through some problems," she answered.

He nodded and folded her close. "Is your aunt going to get worried if we don't emerge from your room for the next two days?" he teased.

Chelsea laughed. "She'll be okay with it. And I can send you out for food."

"You're kidding."

"I'm not sure. I'll let you know in the morning," she promised, then brought his mouth back to hers for a kiss full of passion and promises.

* * * * *

*There's more romance and mystery
to uncover during*
A HOLIDAY MYSTERY AT JENKINS COVE!
*Don't miss the next compelling story,
CHRISTMAS AWAKENING
by Ann Voss Peterson
on sale in November 2008.
Only from Harlequin Intrigue!*

Here's a sneak peek at
THE CEO'S CHRISTMAS PROPOSITION,
the first in USA TODAY *bestselling author*
Merline Lovelace's
HOLIDAYS ABROAD *trilogy*
coming in November 2008.

American Devon McShay is about to get the
Christmas surprise of a lifetime when she
meets her new client, sexy billionaire Caleb
Logan, for the very first time.

Silhouette®

Desire

Available November 2008

Her breath whistled out in a sigh of relief when he exited Customs. Devon recognized him right away from the newspaper and magazine articles her friend and partner Sabrina had looked up during her frantic prep work.

Caleb John Logan, Jr. Thirty-one. Six-two. With jet-black hair, laser-blue eyes and a linebacker's shoulders under his charcoal-gray cashmere overcoat. His jaw-dropping good looks didn't score him any points with Devon. She'd learned the hard way not to trust handsome heartbreakers like Cal Logan.

But he was a client. An important one. And she was willing to give someone who'd served a hitch in the marines before earning a B.S. from the University of Oregon, an MBA from Stanford and his first million at the ripe old age of twenty-six the benefit of the doubt.

Right up until he spotted the hot-pink pashmina, that is.

Devon knew the flash of color was more visible than the sign she held up with his name on it. So she wasn't surprised when Logan picked her out of the crowd and cut in her direction. She'd just plastered on her best businesswoman smile when he whipped an arm around her waist. The next moment she was sprawled against his cashmere-covered chest.

"Hello, brown eyes."

Swooping down, he covered her mouth with his.

Sheer astonishment kept Devon rooted to the spot for a few seconds while her mind whirled chaotically. Her first thought was that her client had downed a few too many drinks during the long flight. Her second, that he'd mistaken the kind of escort and consulting services her company provided. Her third shoved everything else out of her head.

The man could kiss!

His mouth moved over hers with a skill that ignited sparks at a half dozen flash points throughout her body. Devon hadn't experienced that kind of spontaneous combustion in a while. A *long* while.

The sparks were still popping when she pushed off his chest, only now they fueled a flush of anger.

"Do you always greet women you don't know with a lip-lock, Mr. Logan?"

A smile crinkled the skin at the corners of his eyes. "As a matter of fact, I don't. That was from Don."

"Huh?"

"He said he owed you one from New Year's Eve two years ago and made me promise to deliver it."

She stared up at him in total incomprehension. Logan hooked a brow and attempted to prompt a nonexistent memory.

"He abandoned you at the Waldorf. Five minutes before midnight. To deliver twins."

"I don't have a clue who or what you're…"

Understanding burst like a water balloon.

"Wait a sec. Are you talking about Sabrina's old boyfriend? Your buddy, who's now an ob-gyn doc?"

It was Logan's turn to look startled. He recovered faster than Devon had, though. His smile widened into a rueful grin.

"I take it you're not Sabrina Russo."

"No, Mr. Logan, I am *not*."

* * * * *

Be sure to look for
THE CEO'S CHRISTMAS PROPOSITION
by Merline Lovelace.
Available in November 2008
wherever books are sold,
including most bookstores, supermarkets,
drugstores and discount stores.

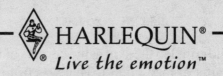

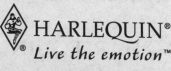

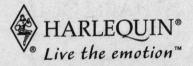

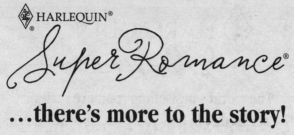
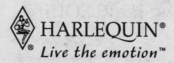

HARLEQUIN®
Presents

The world's bestselling romance series...
The series that brings you your favorite authors,
month after month:

Helen Bianchin...Emma Darcy
Lynne Graham...Penny Jordan
Miranda Lee...Sandra Marton
Anne Mather...Carole Mortimer
Melanie Milburne...Michelle Reid

and many more talented authors!

Wealthy, powerful, gorgeous men...
Women who have feelings just like your own...
The stories you love, set in exotic, glamorous locations...

HARLEQUIN®
Presents

Seduction and Passion Guaranteed!

Harlequin® Historical
Historical Romantic Adventure!

Imagine a time of chivalrous knights and unconventional ladies, roguish rakes and impetuous heiresses, rugged cowboys and spirited frontierswomen— these rich and vivid tales will capture your imagination!

Harlequin Historical . . . they're too good to miss!

Silhouette

SPECIAL EDITION™

Emotional, compelling stories that capture the intensity of living, loving and creating a family in today's world.

Special Edition features bestselling authors such as Susan Mallery, Sherryl Woods, Christine Rimmer, Joan Elliott Pickart— and many more!

For a romantic, complex and emotional read, choose Silhouette Special Edition.

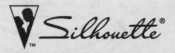